The Hollywood Girl

A Mulholland Diaries Novel

By

L'vette Sonai

DAISY SCOUT

PUBLISHING

Nashville ~ Los Angeles

This is a work of fiction. With the exception of passing references to real celebrities, all characters are entirely imagined and any resemblance to real persons or events is purely coincidental. Although reference is made to real celebrities, establishments and events, the contexts in which they are portrayed are all products of the author's imagination.

The Hollywood Girl

First Edition ©2013 L'vette Sonai

ISBN-13: 978-0-692-26041-8
Daisy Scout Publishing

Author photo by Tiffany Helmick

Dear Reader,

I want to thank you for sharing in this wonderful journey. It is your encouragement and support that fuels my desire to tell the stories of the fabulous women and men featured in the Mulholland Diaries series. It has been quite a ride.

So, sit back, relax and enjoy!

L'vette Sonai xo

THE HOLLYWOOD GIRL

Prologue

Golden Globes flashback

I had begun to hate award shows. It wasn't that I didn't fancy getting all dressed up in the latest couture and partying at A-list soirées afterwards. That was the fun part. It's the facade I had to keep up, that was getting old. The entire *Hi Doll...let's do lunch next week...You look incredible...kiss-kiss* A parade of the same old parties and the same old restaurants. Hollywood had become a tired cliché.

"Here we go. Are you ready, Alex?"

The limo came to a slow roll and I could hear muffled screeches from the crowd and the demanding shouts of the paparazzi. Our driver opened the door and right on cue, Hayden Jones, my Golden Globe nominated husband, removed his sunglasses and painted on that smile I had fallen in love with in the beginning and now had grown to despise.

"Yes, my love."

With a submissive gleam in my eyes, I gulped back my favorite champagne and rubbed my hand against the fabric of the backless, and fleshy sequined gown I'd chosen from my closet just that afternoon. I had purchased the dress a month before, just in case Hayden was nominated – and he was.

Hayden got out first. "Cheer up, baby..." He gently grabbed my hand and helped me out. Kissing my cheek, which induced the uproar around us, he continued, "...every girl out there wishes she were in your shoes." Looking out, with his dimples framing that million dollar smile, he waved at his adoring fans.

I thought, oh really? We continued down the red carpet, waving and dancing for the audience. I turned to him with a smile on my face and contempt in my eyes. "Well, maybe one of them will get lucky, like I did." I squeezed his hand. "Smile for the cameras."

"Alexia! Alexia, who are you wearing? This way Alexia! You look beautiful!" The photographers were shouting my name from all directions.

Arching my back, with a glance over my shoulder, I gave them what they wanted. "Thank you... Armani Privé!"

I was bound to end up on one of those fashion lists the next day. That over-stretched fashion cop ripped me to shreds after the Emmys, so I thought I'd give her something extra special to dish about this time. The girls were pushed up and on full display. And thanks to whatever I popped into my champagne glass in the limo, I didn't much care about anything else.

The blinding flashes were sending me into an even worse frame of mind. Once again, there I was, carrying out my duties as the perfect Hollywood wife. I took a moment, handing the paparazzi a gift wrapped smile and what the press described as bedroom eyes. Everyone knew it was me who made Hayden look like a real power player on that red carpet. We were Hollywood eye candy.

I'm Alexia Diamond, and I've grown a lifetime away from being that small town girl who rolled into Los Angeles nearly ten years ago. Back then, at twenty-two years old, all I had was two hundred dollars to my name and big dreams of becoming a celebrity makeup artist. I soon discovered that LA wasn't Barstow and I was forced to wise up, real fast.

I learned early on that my wide-eyed sweetness and subtle seduction, was like Kryptonite to men. Couple that with the fact that money was so tight in the beginning, having to go back home to that desert pit constantly loomed before me. But I'd be damned if I went back there. I had to concoct a sure-fire plan and with the quickness. I did and it all worked out in the long run. But boy, did I take some hard knocks along the way.

Thinking back, I know I sold my soul. You have to be willing to make tough choices when you want this life. I tried to stay a step ahead of the game. Eventually I got it all: the money, the mansions and the first class lifestyle. Still, the sad part is, no one has discovered that underneath this pretty facade are irreparable wounds.

Maybe if I share my story, I can spare the next naive princess who comes off the bus from Barstow.

Let's give her a try and start from the beginning, shall we?

*M*y heart always beat to a symphony and

danced to the tune of elegance and Hollywood parties.

Don't call me Barstow, I screamed.

I never fit with the regulars.

Maybe I should have.

My dreams were too lofty, they said.

Perhaps they were right.

No sooner than I was able to grasp hold of the

colorful fairytale I longed for,

it was smashed and I nearly lost myself.

Next time, I'll dream in black and white. That way at

least, I can continue my dance with Illusion.

Reality, as it turned out, was too much for me to

handle.

This is dedicated to you.

Signed,

The Hollywood Girl xo

ACT I: *Hollywood and the Single Girl*
"Welcome to Hollywood..."

Don't call me Barstow

$\mathcal{N}$othing got under my skin more than the military guys who came into Bob's Café during the lunch rush. They ate a ton of food, and were extremely demanding; like I was their personal cook. I was just a waitress, and a certain group of them always asked for me. "We want that one to help us." *That one* Who did they think they were? These guys were always raising their bushy eyebrows and winking at me, like they were God's gift, just because they wore military uniforms. But, to some of the locals they were like movie stars.

On Friday nights, the Base Head girls (a nickname given by yours truly) would cruise the perimeter of the military base, waiting to be chosen. They'd end up at The Desert Palm hotel; sometimes not even making it into the rooms. My friends and I have spotted girls taking turns giving blow jobs next to the dumpsters. Then I would hear them the next day in the café, bragging and giggling about their soldier boys. Whatever! They gave it away for free. Complete trash.

Dot, who managed Bob's, was really protective of me. She knew I was over that town, and was subject to take off my apron and high-tail it right out of there. Every day I wanted to quit. I love her because she got me that job as a favor to my mother. Even so, I didn't want to be stuck at Bob's forever. I had goals that didn't end in Barstow. I got good grades at junior college, where I studied cosmetology and never stop planning my escape from the desert. I knew I couldn't stay there or I would end up giving free facials at the department store for the rest of my life. Dot used to call me Little Dreamer, because I would always talk about living in Los Angeles. *When I get to LA…and …someday, I'll be living the life Dot, you'll see!*

It was going to happen. I just didn't know how to get there. At the least, I was going to get out of that town and finally live among people who were more like me. I felt like a big city girl who was stuck in Mayberry USA. Then one day, while flipping through a fashion magazine…it hit me. It was clear what my calling was.

I had always been the go-to when you wanted your face made up perfectly. So what'd I do? I applied to the Esthetique Institute in Los Angeles. After years of being the go-to for makeup during Homecoming weeks and proms, it was no surprise that I got accepted. I now had to find a place to live. One of the administrators helped me find an apartment and a roommate. My father was the lifesaver. He made me promise to do my best and to focus on my goal, and with that…he would pay my half of the rent up to a year. After that, I should have a suitable job. He also made me promise not to say a word to my mother about our agreement.

That August I packed my bags - all three of them - and headed to the big city on the Greyhound. I didn't know a soul in LA besides my roommate Lilly, and that was thanks to a few phone conversations. I sensed that Lilly was a little more street smart than me. She was from Las Vegas and ran off to LA to get away from her crazy boyfriend who was a bouncer at a strip club. I got the feeling that's how they met: at the strip club. Out of courtesy, I chose not to confirm that hunch.

Lilly Fields had been in LA six months before I got there. While working at the Bloomingdale's beauty counter at the Beverly Center, her manager suggested she go to the Institute because she had real skills. Lilly had porcelain-like skin and her makeup was always flawless. I agree that she had been wasting her time peddling six dollar lip gloss. One thing I caught onto immediately was that this girl didn't play. Her razor sharp wit was the buffer for cut throat determination to make it. *In it to win it* was her motto, and she was.

I arrived at the apartment off Main Street downtown, on a Thursday afternoon. I had no idea what to expect out of my roomie.

"I hope I'm not rooming with Lizzie Borden." I giggle as I knocked on the door before entering the apartment. It was a dull brick building in the fashion district; an easy sprint to the Institute. I loved the location because it felt like being in New York. Not that I had ever been. "Hello? Lilly are you in here?"

"Well, hey there, Barstow!"

Lilly stood in the kitchen, pouring a soft drink into a glass, waiting for a response. I remember being surprised at how sweet she looked, though I knew better.

I sighed in mock frustration. "Please, don't call me that!" I put my bags down and hugged her. It was a relief to be starting my new life with a friend who didn't think jean cutoffs and boots, was dressing up. "Oh, the rest of my stuff is with the taxi. He's not even helping, can you believe it?"

"Actually, I can. Come on, I'll help you."

Lilly swooped up her long blonde hair into a ponytail, tugged at her linen shorts that hugged her tiny butt and bolted out the door. She was a go-getter kind of girl. I could see that.

We spent that first night talking and swapping stories about bad boyfriends and fake friends. I was an expert on the topics. Though we were just getting to know each other, we knew we would be friends for a long time. I rarely met a girl I liked being around. Lilly was the coolest white chick I'd ever met. Being twenty-three, she treated me like a little sister and I trusted her.

We swore from that night on, to always have each other's back.

Flirting starts in ten

"How long before you come out of the bathroom, Alex?"

Lilly stood outside the door, getting on my last nerve. I was on my period and suffering crazy cramps, sitting on the side of the tub. The last thing I needed was for her to be yelling at me about her date being on his way.

"Lilly, please! Damn…" I opened the door. She tried to show empathy, but was really hoping I would get moving. Her hair was messy and eye makeup half done. "Why are you just now getting ready, anyways?"

"I know, Alex. I just had to finish one last step for the practice exam tomorrow." She fumbled through the drawer on her side of the vanity. Where is that Chanel compact I just…ah, here it is!" Lilly did a speed run of a smoky eye in thirty seconds flat.

"Well, you look cute. You should keep your hair down, though."

She glanced up at my reflection in the mirror. "Yeah?"

"Here, I'll do it."

Lilly was so flustered over this guy coming and I wanted to help her out. It was the least I could do. She was helpless.

After ten minutes and sweet smelling hair products all over my hands, she was ready. I gave her a simple sleek style. Then we heard the buzzer.

Apparently she'd met this guy at a bookstore at The Grove. She said he was really good looking and "not at all like my ex." *Right* I thought. We always say that.

Now, I didn't know what her boyfriend back in Vegas looked like, but this one was dangerously cute. Guys like him don't wander around alone in bookstores. Do they?

"Hi, you're Jerzy, right?" I loved his name and the way Lilly pronounced it… *Jerrr-zee*. He was cute in an intentionally rugged kind of way. From his dark, strategically groomed hair and sideburns that hit just above his jaw line – he was hot.

Jerzy extended his hand, giving me the once-over. "Yes, and you're…Alexia."

Watching his appraisal of our surroundings and the way he confidently watched me as I handed him bottled water, I knew he was a smooth operator. I figured he was at least twenty-five and judging by his wardrobe, Jerzy wasn't broke.

"Alexia, how do you like LA, so far?" He twisted the top off and took a light sip. He had nice lips.

"I love it, thanks."

Lilly needed to hurry because I was tired of feeling obligated to engage her friend. Plus, he was the type that would have encouraged me to start flirting with him in another ten seconds. The look in his eyes told me he wouldn't mind.

"Hi, Jerzy!"

Lilly entered the room. She looked adorable in the jewel blue silk blouse and black skirt that hit right above her knees. Her four inch pumps complimented her legs. I silently approved.

Leaning against the wall, I joked, "You make sure you have her back at a decent hour, Jerzy."

It was a chilly February night. While Jerzy helped Lilly with her jacket, he craned his head around her shoulder and winked at me saying he would. I looked away quickly, sending him a strong No. If he knew what was good for him, he'd stop right there, with whatever he was *thinking* he might get away with.

I went to the window and watched them pull off in the black Mercedes parked out front. "Not bad, Jerzy."

~

Lilly woke me just after midnight when she dropped her handbag on the wood floor. I yelled towards the hallway. "Lilly?"

"Yeah, it's me. Sorry!"

The apartment was cold. I climbed out of bed,

tiptoeing across the floor in nothing but a tank top and panties. I leaned into the doorway across from mine. "So what did you guys do, Lil?"

"We had dinner at a beautiful little restaurant named Lillian's, overlooking the ocean in Malibu. He said it was in honor of my name. Isn't that cute?" She rambled on and on like a wound up doll. It was so out of character, but a little amusing. "Oh, and you'll never guess who sat near us? Pam Anderson! She's a lot more real looking in person. Jerzy was so sweet, he introduced me to her." Even in the dark, I could see Lilly's glowing excitement. That wasn't a good sign because it meant she was into him already.

I hoped Jerzy was not a game player and wouldn't break Lilly's heart. One of us had to think clearly, because she had fallen fast. I hoped I would never fall like that.

"Aw, honey I'm excited for you..." I yawned on cue. "...but we'll talk more in the morning."

On the way back into bed, I thought *finally a guy who doesn't think Red Lobster is fine dining.* Pulling the covers up to my neck, I settled back into my well earned sleep.

One in my size?

"So are you coming with us, Alex? It's a fund raiser at this chi-chi mansion in Beverly Hills and you need to meet some interesting people. Jerzy insisted that I invite you. There's bound to be somebody famous there. It'll be fun." Lilly wouldn't let up.

I was hesitant about tagging along as a third wheel. It always made me feel bad. Especially now since Lilly and Jerzy were a real couple by this time.

"I don't know. I was thinking I'd pick up dinner and order a movie." I looked forward to snuggling under a blanket and watching a good romantic comedy.

"What? No - it's Saturday night!" Lilly smacked my butt with the face towel she was holding.

"Stop! Seriously, I'm good."

She just gazed at me and then hopped up on the bathroom counter. "Okay listen, I really want you to go. I think you'll have a good time. He may even have a friend who is just your size."

I looked her up and down, "What size would that be? At least eight inches or it's a waste." We burst into laughter. "Okay I'll go, but only to shut you up."

"Good! Let's go pick out dresses. We have to glam it up. It's Beverly Hills, Dahhhling…" She mockingly leaned her head back in a pose. "Come on, we only have an hour to get ready."

Truth was, it was about time I got out and really enjoy Los Angeles and what it had to offer. What better place to start than Beverly Hills?

You ever get that feeling?

*T*he Mercedes drove through the most intimidating gates I'd ever seen. It almost felt invasive, only I knew we were on the list. As we entered the estate, Jerzy announced, "Welcome to Greystone, ladies." It was just about seven o'clock and the grounds were dark but you could still see the lush hills as we continued up the drive. "This is a beautiful property. You'll love it."

I started to feel the same jitters I did on prom night back in Barstow. All dressed up and you can't wait to show off your outfit. "What is this benefiting again?"

Lilly's head flung around. "The Children's Hospital." Her voice sounded very proud of that fact. She comfortably placed her hand on the back of Jerzy's seat, as she continued on. I admit...they looked good together.

"Oh, that's great!" I started to feel more enthused about the evening.

Jerzy's car approached the roundabout and stopped. The valet opened our doors. I got out, looking around at the pretty faces and hoping that I fit in and not look like that third wheel all night. I came prepared to hold my own, among the glamorous crowd, wearing a purple, fitted BCBG cowl neck dress that gave me just enough cleavage without being obvious. I draped my shawl and handbag over my arm as we made our way inside.

I could tell someone was watching me. You ever get that feeling? Looking around, I found a gorgeous set of eyes peering in my direction. I was too caught off to be impressed. Though I admit, he was intriguing.

"Lilly, who's that guy over there? Do you know him?" I held my champagne flute close to my lips to conceal my words.

Not one for discretion, Lilly tilted her head to peer past me. "Who, that hot guy standing near the window? No, but do *you* want to?"

"No, Lilly. I was just asking. He's staring and it makes me a little nervous."

"Well he's smiling in this direction, and it's not at me. Stop playing hard to get, Alex. Smile back!" Just in the nick of time, Jerzy summoned her over to the group he was chatting with. Lilly let out a frustrating sigh, tucked her Fendi clutch under her arm and sashayed off in his direction. She looked back at me with a mischievous grin.

I turned towards the bar and continued nursing my drink, checking out the glitterati crowd that had turned out for the fundraiser. I wasn't in the mood to be singled out by anyone. I just wanted to enjoy the party.

After a half hour of mingling and enjoying cocktails, we made our way onto the terrace where dinner was served. Jerzy held out an arm for each of us and guided us to our table. That's one thing I'll give him, Jerzy was very classy. He knew I felt like the odd girl out, but wanted to make sure I wouldn't feel that way for long. As I sat in my chair and was about to scoot it forward, I was interrupted.

"Allow me." I looked up and there was Mr. Handsome from across the room. Wouldn't you know, he was sitting at our table? I wondered what Jerzy had done to maneuver that situation.

Jerzy came up behind him, patting his shoulder, "You two have met, I see."

I glared at Jerzy, behind Mr. Handsome's back. I wanted to both curse him and hug him at the same time. Jerzy knew what he was doing.

After a very awkward few seconds of my set-up gazing at me with a sexy smirk and me saying absolutely nothing, he introduced himself. "I'm Erik, and you are..."

I wondered where he was from. His accent was faint, but I could tell he wasn't American. I'd find out later he was South African.

"Alexia...but, call me Alex." I couldn't contain my blushing smile.

Tanned, gray eyes and dark brown hair...Erik was yummy. Not to mention, he seemed nice, and the conversation was good. He told me about what brought him to the states. His family divided time between South Africa and New York.

"I decided I wanted to explore Los Angeles. New York can be a bore. What about you?"

"Me? Let's see..."

Of course, I told him my earth-shattering story of escaping Barstow for life in the City of Angels. As intently as he listened, you would have thought I was sharing the great secret to world peace. I had almost forgotten that Lilly and Jerzy were seated with us. I could have sat there talking with Erik all night.

When I woke up the next morning, I felt oddly refreshed and happy. Like I was being me for the first time since I'd gotten to Los Angeles.

"Good morning, pretty girl..." *How can he still look like this in the morning?*

Yes - I spent the night with Erik. What? Sometimes a girl lives for the moment. Men haven't cornered the market on that. I know it's not right. I normally wouldn't have done such a thing, but when I left

Greystone with him and ended up in the super exclusive Malibu Colony, something switched in me. I felt like finally, a man wanted to show me a nice time, the way I knew I deserved. I had put up with a lot of nonsense before I got to LA. So, I didn't feel bad about being with Erik.

We drank expensive champagne, shared some laughs, drank more champagne and...well, what can I say?

Lying on your back, looking up at the ceiling of a luxurious beach house can be an aphrodisiac.

Where I fit

"*A*lex, this is a fantastic opportunity. You should be excited about it!"

Lilly was right, but I was a nervous wreck. It was July, we'd just passed the State exam and I was about to meet with the Lorena Maldono Agency. Lorena represents the nation's top makeup artists and hairstylists and she had two spots open. I was scouted by one of her representatives and for lack of better words, was told: "Don't screw up your chance. You only get one shot to prove you're it!" No pressure there. I had to get in. My job at Sephora had become a stalled existence. Not to mention, my money was running low.

So what about Lilly, you ask? Well, she was offered the chance to go to New York and work with a famous makeup artist to the stars. She was offered - but turned it down. I couldn't believe it and was so vocal in my opinion.

Remember Jerzy? Well, he popped the question. No - not to marry him, but to move into his Hollywood Hills pad. She jumped in, head first. Supposedly they were madly in love, but I think he wanted to keep a tight leash on her. Lilly bragged that she was so good in bed, that he became obsessed with her. A tiger like Lilly would be hard to tame long distance. On the flip side, she knew that if she left for New York, some hot little spinner would take her place before she boarded the plane.

Jerzy Freidland was the quintessential trust fund baby. His father is Bernard "Bernie" Freidland, the head of Paramax Motion Pictures. That meant his bankroll was long and he wasn't stingy with it, especially when it came to the ladies. Jerzy had made Lilly an offer he knew she wouldn't dare pass up. She told me, "I'm getting it while the gettin's good!" That's just what she said. Lilly knew Jerzy's undying lust for her would last until either he or she got tired. The Jerzy Freidlands of the world don't cry over women for long. So, Lilly moved in with him, without hesitation.

Meanwhile, I met with Lorena Maldano on a Tuesday afternoon, at her West Hollywood offices. Twenty minutes into our meeting, she offered to represent me. I accepted and couldn't wait to get started. I was finally going to be doing what I had dreamt of my whole life. To have Lorena Maldano as my mentor was like the golden cherry on top.

Thank God gigs were fairly steady because now, I was paying my own way. I also knew I wanted to move closer to the Westside. In early summer I found a place I could afford; a two bedroom apartment on Rossmore Avenue, just off Wilshire Boulevard. It was in a great location in Hancock Park and was really cute, except the bathroom was painted a horrible olive green. Most importantly though, it was all mine.

There were some colorful characters in that art deco building. First you had old Mrs. Simmons, an heiress of some sort, who was almost eighty and lived on the first floor. Why she chose apartment living over a nice tuck away in the hills still baffles me. There were also the two fabulously chic boys on the fifth floor. I met them in the elevator when I was moving in. Rob and Sam gave me the skinny on all the things and people to avoid. They failed to warn me that they themselves would keep up so much noise that I'd hardly get any sleep at night. Though they would take me out in West Hollywood and show me off as they said, I still hold a grudge against them for the late night partying. A girl needs her beauty rest.

Last but not least, there was Monet Caprice. I was sure from the start that was not her real name, but I never let on. I just rolled with it. She was a bombshell of a brunette with the prettiest brown skin. Monet supposedly was born in Montreal and moved to Los

Angeles as a teenager with her mother in the Nineties, just after her parents divorced. She did have a slight French accent, but Monet was an "actress", so who really knows? Her place was decked out in fine contemporary décor. Not cheap inspirations, but tasteful chairs, fresh flowers, expensive place settings and impressive replicas on the walls. Monet also drove a late model BMW. This girl was always at home, so I wondered how she could afford it all.

"Alex, there are people in this town who want to sponsor up and coming talent. They are like…investors. You see?"

Oh yes, Monet. I saw.

Miss Caprice

*O*n the world of celebrity girlfriends, women sleep with one eye on their man, and the other on the woman next to him. The innocent often don't see what's right in front of them. The competition is cut throat, but there's still a level of respect. An unspoken code, if you will.

I won't take your man. I just let him know an upgrade is available. It's up to you to block him from ever seeing me coming. If he leaves you, it's your own lazy fault.

Monet Caprice was that girl. You never wanted to let her within five hundred feet of your man, especially if he was famous. She was a sugar daddy magnet; sometimes even A-list sugar mammas took the bait. Not one to discriminate, rarely did Monet turn an offer down. It was about "...getting my money!" as she so greedily would say in that deliberate accent. She always got her money. Monet was very discreet and had few friends; none of whom she trusted. I kept her close to keep a strong eye on her. If you learn the plays, you recognize the signs.

You'll see what I mean later.

The three thousand dollar kiss

$\mathcal{L}$illy called me on a Friday afternoon saying she wanted to see my new apartment. When she showed up, I could tell she was sincerely happy for me. With her prized Chanel tote slung over her shoulder, she strolled from room to room, all four of them.

"So Lilly how are things... with Jerzy I mean?" I was in the kitchen making black tea for us. Lilly plopped down on the overstuffed chair which was intentionally placed in a cozy corner of the room that was framed by two wall length windows. I used to love sitting in that window, reading and watching people go by. I was blessed to have gotten a corner apartment. It doesn't get better than that. I sat our tea on the coffee table and settled in, because I saw in her eyes that she was about to lay something on me. "Well? Are you and Mr. Wonderful all cozy up in the hills?" I teased, sipping my scorching hot tea which burned my tongue. "Ouch, be careful girl, the tea is hot."

Lilly glanced down at her cup, "We're great. And Jerzy...Alex, I'm never letting him go!" As she giggled, I could see in her demeanor that wild child Lilly from Vegas was tucked away. This new girl was lighter. The tough exterior was fading. She was obviously enjoying ingesting Jerzy's million dollar lifestyle. It worried me a little.

"Oh really? It's that good, huh?" I glanced over her, admiring her Manolos, which I used to lust after ever since they were shoved down our throats by actresses and so-called socialites around the globe. Lilly was living the dream and she really hadn't done anything to earn it. "Well he certainly looks good on you."

Nodding her head, and looking out of the window onto the street below, she asked, "Speaking of, I heard Erik and you have been pret-ty friendly lately." I knew she was phishing.

The night I met Erik Mahron at the fundraiser at Greystone Mansion, was a curious situation in every sense. I mean, we obviously were attracted to each other from the word Go. Then I found out our meeting was not a casual run-in. He was a buddy of Jerzy. Before dessert that evening, Lilly and I excused ourselves to the ladies room, like girls do. She wasted not a moment rolling off his credentials.

"He's single, rich, and comes from good family...you know Chandler Mahron, the actress? Yeah- that's Erik's sister!" She went on and on. By the time we finished fluffing our over-sprayed hair, Erik was a saint. I safely assumed he

was a decent guy. Not some cad preying on what he perceived as naivety. I could assume that, right?

Erik and I talked through dessert; neither of us really touching the chocolate soufflé. Well, I ran a finger through the vanilla sauce and licked it right in front of him. It was to die for. I remember him stumbling over his words, watching me.

"Um, yeah he's cool. I enjoy his company." Lilly raised her eyebrow and pursed her lips. I giggled, "What?" I reached for my tea in a hurry.

"Well, he digs you, for sure!" *Digs me?* Lilly had discovered a whole new vocabulary.

"We had fun that night, that's it Lil. He's nice, but…"

Lilly seemed to be irritated by that. "Yes he is, and he can do a lot for you."

He did do a lot for me. He's a beast in the sack and gave me what I wanted, just when I needed it. When I woke up the morning after the party, he let me sleep in and later took me home to change before Sunday brunch at The Ivy. Erik said he wanted to see me again, but only if *I* wanted.

So, what was wrong with him? Because there's always something wrong with them.

That night I found three grand in my wallet, wrapped in a note written on monogrammed rice paper. *You're a delicious kisser. P.S. Rodeo Drive was designed with you in mind…go enjoy it!*

Stunned, I called Erik. "I'm not a whore, you sonofabitch!" I kept interrupting him while he tried to apologize and explain that he meant it as a gift. Saying he wanted to take me shopping but sensed I wouldn't let him. I still don't know if I buy that, but I sure as hell didn't give the money back.

Lilly bringing up Erik hit a nerve. "Why are you pressing the issue, Lilly? Erik and I are fine just the way things are."

I didn't want to be tied down. My career was taking off, and I preferred to be free to meet whomever I wanted and do whatever I wanted. Possessive boyfriends never did it for me. It's like Lilly wanted me to be a trophy girl the way she now was.

I did see Erik again. And, as fate or whatever you choose, would have it, I learned a lot about what I wanted as well as what I deserved in life, because of him.

He would prove to not only be my occasional lover, but a friend. He taught me to never give anything away for free, not even my heart. He said: "That's how these girls screw themselves out here. Just make sure you always take care of yourself, Doll Face."

I laughed when he said that, because it reminded me

of all of the dumb Base Head girls back in Barstow who gave it away for free.

Erik needn't worry about me. I was a quick study and was beginning to see Tinsletown in a whole new light.

Doctor, Doctor

$\mathcal{M}$onet called as I was walking through the door one Friday afternoon. I believe it was early July. She had a date with a gentleman who had offered to cook dinner. Monet asked if she could bring a friend along; I being that friend. Of course I was suspicious initially, but she told me he was a neurologist and I pulled up his name in the hospital directory to verify it. I know that was odd, but I figured we were safe with him, because he wasn't about to flip on us and risk his reputation. The plans were dinner and a movie - in his home theater.

The minute we drove through the guarded entrance of The Summit off Mulholland Drive, I knew Monet's guy was not *just* some neurologist. You couldn't roll wheels past those gates unless you were prepared to smack down at least three million. We got there just after seven and the gate to his home was open, so we parked and let ourselves in.

"Monet, you said *he's* cooking?" I looked around the warm great room that welcomed us. Whoever this man was, he had good taste. Not overdone, but elegant. "I like him already."

"I told you, he's amazing..." She gushed, "...and wait until you see *him*." Catching a glimpse of herself in the foyer mirror, Monet smoothed the flyaway strands of her lush, dark brown mane that brushed against her dewy skin, and reached into her bag for a lip gloss quickly swiping it across her inflated lips.

Monet was a seductress and she knew how to use what she had.

Just then Dr. Geoffrey Mark popped up. *Doctors don't look like this in Barstow. At least mine didn't.* I tried not to seem eager to be introduced. He was drying his hands with a dish towel, and then flung it over his shoulder. "Hello ladies..." His smile was beautiful. I remember that clearly.

Monet gave him a hug, kissing both of his cheeks. "Geoffrey, please meet my friend, Alexia. We live together, I mean in the same building." It was like she really needed him to approve of me. Not that it mattered.

He checked me out, giving a smooth once-over while extending his hand, "It's nice to meet you, Alexia."

"My pleasure, Dr. Mark."

"Call me Geoffrey, please."

Gesturing towards the huge open living room, he told us to make ourselves at home, and that dinner was almost ready. He glanced back at Monet, giving her a look like he wanted to eat her up right then and there. I admit, she was sexy and it exuded from her like heat.

Now before I go any further, I need to queue you in on Dr. Geoffrey. He was really good looking. Not movie star looks, but very handsome, and that's not a compliment I hand out so easily. A man's got to earn it, and he did. At fifty, he had a fit body, nice eyes and delicious brown skin. Not to mention the graying temples. That did it for me; feeding my older man fetish, and all.

We had dinner in the dining room, which overlooked the canyon.

"So Doc...excuse me, Geoffrey, you've probably had more than a few celebrity patients, huh?" I sipped my wine hoping he'd name drop.

He just softly chuckled. "A few..."

"Right..." I nodded at his discretion.

"Oh you're being modest!" Monet turned to me. "I'm sure half of Hollywood would be six feet under if it weren't for him." She was clearly tipsy. I acted as if I wasn't that interested. I knew the doctor wouldn't name names.

In the middle of the only Steven Segal movie I've ever enjoyed, Monet got up from the ultra suede lounger and sat next to Dr. Geoffrey. They whispered, or rather she did, as she rubbed the collar of his shirt with her fingernail. I couldn't help but think she looked hungry and desperate. The scene made me want to leave.

Monet blurted, out of nowhere, "Alex, let's check out the hot tub, yes? It's fabulous!" She bounced up, tugging at the crotch of her skinny jeans. I was amused by the way Monet turned into a little girl right before my eyes; baby voice and all. I looked at her like *are you crazy?* It was chilly out and I wasn't interested.

That was, until Dr. Geoffrey invited me to, and... I didn't want to appear rude.

"I have a few calls to make, but please, enjoy the spa."

The wine hit me fast and that usually loosened my inhibitions.

Monet tapped my leg and gestured. "Come with me."

As we walked down the hallway on the lower level, I could see ahead out the glass door to the pool. She ducked into the guestroom and grabbed robes and towels from the bath.

"You do realize we are skinny dipping?" Her expression was so matter of fact. "I didn't bring a suit, did you?"

"What? Of course not, how could I have known that

we...?" I sat down on the bench at the foot of the bed, frustrated with her game playing.

Dr. Geoffrey stopped at the doorway with his Blackberry in hand. "There you are. Are you ready?"

I was nervous, but curious. Here I was, agreeing to strip naked in front of a complete stranger. As logic would roam in my fuzzy head, he was a medical professional. That was the justification. A naked body was just that to him - a body. Monet wasn't shy at all. I wouldn't have expected her to be. She stepped out of her jeans and pulled her top over her head, baring her nakedness while tip-toeing all the way out the door and dove into the pool.

Needless to say, I enjoyed myself. The pool with its built-in spa tub was at the ideal elevation so as to view the lights below. While Dr. Geoffrey was swimming a lap, I soaked in the atmosphere. Monet made her way out of and settled onto a chaise. I got out a few minutes later. Grabbing a robe and lifting my hair from underneath the collar, I caught Dr. Geoffrey watching me. I quickly pulled it closed.

"Geoffrey, this is fantastic, thank you!"

He nodded, "My pleasure. I'm enjoying the company." Then he climbed out of the pool... wearing swim trunks. Men play so unfairly!

Glancing back at Monet, who was now passed out in the chair, I was concerned about her sleeping in the night air.

"She can't stay here like this. Is there somewhere...?"

"Of course. Let's get her inside."

Dr. Geoffrey opened the door while I sat at Monet's feet and woke her, talking her in. She finally stood, mumbling something as we made our way to the guest room, where she climbed into bed.

I knew we'd be there for the night.

Dr. Geoffrey went back outside and I followed. The stars were beautiful and I just wanted to gaze at them. It made me long for those calm nights in Barstow. Just for a second, it did.

"Do you come out here a lot?"

"Not really. I'm so busy, that it's hard to find time." He seemed amused that I was in awe of it. "You're a lovely young woman, Alexia. I'm glad Monet brought you."

I smiled back, wrapping the robe around my bare thighs. "Thank you. Me too."

What he said next shocked me.

The good doctor had an eager look in his eyes as he hesitated. "Would you let me finish that?"

I looked around. "Excuse me... finish what?" I was completely lost.

He sat up and leaned towards me, and whispered, "Your cute little strip. Let me finish shaving it."

It was at that moment I realized he had indeed seen my meticulously shaved bikini area. I didn't know what to say, but I thanked God I *had* shaved. "Umm…" I tried laughing it off. He was serious and I was both freaked out and enticed.

"I won't cut you, I promise. I'm pretty careful." I glanced down at his hands - the tools of his profession.

I felt like I was hallucinating. I also admit I was turned on by the idea. "Why would you want to?"

Looking me straight in the eye he admitted, "A lot of men like to shave a woman's legs, but I prefer to use my skills elsewhere. Completely clean is beautiful."

I just stared at him, before… "Okay!" I thought *I can't believe I'm going to let him do this.*

"Don't look so concerned. I think you might enjoy it." He patted my leg and stood up, walking towards the house.

I didn't know if I would, but the experience would certainly be a first for me.

Dr. Geoffrey directed me to the guest room where Monet was sleeping. In the bath, I found a vanity stocked with women's toiletries. Of course, that included an array of perfumes, body lotions, everything a woman needs, including razors. I chose what I always used - the Venus. Obviously there had been many female guests wandering around his hallways.

Walking upstairs to the master suite, I felt like Big Brother was watching. It was by far the craziest thing I'd engaged in to date. I also knew that if I let him do this, there was no telling what else he'd be willing to do. I was only twenty-three years old and a respected surgeon at the top of his field was begging to shave my kitty. What a reverse of power.

"Geoffrey?" I searched the hallway at the top of the stairs. The lights in his bedroom were on and I found him on the bed typing on his laptop. The pool lighting reflected off his balcony. It was like a luxury hotel room.

He glanced up when I entered. "I'm just chatting with my daughter. She's in Boston with her mother." Geoffrey smiled when he spoke of his daughter. He said his goodnights, and reached for my hand. I crawled in next to him, scooting against the headboard. "So, what do you do Alexia?"

"Please call me Alex." At this point, there was no need to be so formal. "I'm an esthetician and makeup artist."

"Very good. Are you on your own, or..." Geoffrey gently pulled me towards him, wrapping his arm around me. He smelled good.

"I'm with an agency. So far things are going very well."

"Really?" He seemed a little surprised that I was serious about a career.

"Yes, it's all pretty exciting."

"Well congratulations. You definitely seem to know where you're headed." His fingertips caressed my shoulder causing a tingle.

I looked around, "Can I use your shower? I want to rinse the chlorine off."

"Off course!" He jumped up and showed me to the master bath. It was huge with gorgeous marble floors, candle stands and plants in every corner."

"I could live in here. It's like a real spa."

"Yeah, but it's a bitch to keep clean. At least that's what my housekeeper says." He chuckled, as he walked out.

"Aha! I didn't think this was a man's doing." I teased him, and then pushed the door closed.

Just as I stepped out of the shower, there was a knock. I wrapped a towel around me, "Come in…"

He leaned against the doorframe. "How was your shower?"

"Perfect!" I smiled, reaching for the Kiehl's body crème on the counter.

Dr. Geoffrey rubbed the back of my shoulders, "May I? Just relax. I won't try anything, I promise."

Why not? "Alright…"

He took the body crème from me, and then grabbed my hand, walking back into the bedroom. I lay on the bed, propped up on my elbows. I should have pumped the breaks, but I couldn't stop. It's like I was dying to know what would happen next. Just like with Erik. Successful men, who have accomplished so much professionally, always have a freaky side. Every second is a curious adventure. I was itching to play along.

'Mmm, this is just what I needed."

I moaned with every stroke of his hands massaging the warm lotion on my skin. It was like every nerve came alive.

"Good, just enjoy it."

Dr. Geoffrey was attentive and careful to add and release pressure just where my body longed for it most. I couldn't have paid for a better experience. I didn't realize certain muscles existed in my body. If he took care of the brain the way he did me, no wonder how he could afford that beautiful mansion.

We became close friends. He wasn't a boyfriend, but more of a confidant I could turn to and hide out with. Whenever I wanted to disappear from the craziness, I ran off to Dr. Geoffrey's.

Monet told me she knew we'd hit it off. He'd already had the wives and the pushy girlfriends, and I made it clear I wasn't looking for that. I wanted him to teach me what I never would have learned from a man my own age. He was someone who gave me just enough attention without being possessive. I knew Geoffrey's job came first, and that's why I stuck around for as long as I did.

He encouraged me to set goals, be the best and leave my mark. To make my own rules and demand they be respected by others. Otherwise a girl like me, from Barstow, would have been eaten alive in Los Angeles.

Dr. Geoffrey is still in my life. I won't pretend we weren't ever sexual. To elude that would be unrealistic, but what he gave me was more than I could have ever asked for.

Oh - and did Dr. Geoffrey carry out his quest that night? Let's just say I'll never look at Gillette the same way again.

Gold Digger Myth

Let's get a couple of things straight, right off. I've never chased after anyone for their money or status. I didn't have to. Only hungry tigers do that.

I also never bought into that gold digger myth. My goals didn't always involve money. Even if they did, you can't judge a girl for doing what *she* feels is necessary. That's being a getter; a survivor. Still, I personally never focused on the money. Some women want the lifestyle and the money of course, is a byproduct. A perk, if you will - lots and lots of perks. Keep reading and you'll understand what I mean.

Women like money. Yet, so do men and they work hard to attain it...because they know women like men *with* money. Especially in Hollywood. It's the dirty, but honest truth.

Why are women tagged as diggers when it all starts with the men? Since the beginning of time men have thought they had to buy women. So they break their backs trying to impress us. They never sit down and ask what *really* makes her happy. Men buy the cars, the homes and the clothes all in hopes of attracting women.

From pimps to drug dealers to the CEOs, they all

work at their craft. They perfect it in hopes of becoming the titans the girls who jilted them before, would now crave. With hard work comes the money and with money comes the power. *That's* when they get the girl of their dreams. They shower her with gifts she never asked for and dangle the good life in front of her so that she'll never want to leave. Then what happens? When she accepts, she's treated as disposable property. The man reminds her that it could all go away if she doesn't follow *his* rules.

She didn't dig for it; it was all bait to get, and hold her hostage. Digging is seeking and she didn't have to search for any of it. It's not fair.

Everything has a price. Your time, your heartache and your loneliness…it all costs. Let's face it, the more lavish your lifestyle the lonelier and insecure a woman becomes. Who would dig for that?

The Gold Digger is a myth.

Besides, for all the tear-stained pillows we sleep on at night, a girl deserves a couple million tucked away underneath that pillow. It softens the blow of reality.

New York, big city of dreams and men

On late January, I left LA for New York Fashion Week. We were to be there for three days, and I was frantic with anticipation. Lorena thought it would be better for me to do the shows instead of being stuck in the rotation of doing makeup for reality-TV stars, so she invited me to the big show. I got called in for a sit-down about my career and where I wanted to take it.

"I chose you because you're smart, hard working and beautiful, and people enjoy being around you. So, I've decided..." I cringed when said that, like my fate lie in her hands. "... to let you weigh your options. Get your feet really wet, so to speak."

My options? I thought for sure Lorena was trying to get rid of me already. I was wrong; just the opposite, in fact. She stood up from behind her Lucite desk, smoothed her slender hips with her hands and declared in her Colombian accent: "You need to go to New York, my dear."

I shifted in my seat, crossing my legs, trying to relax. "You're sending me to Fashion Week? Oh, Lorena!" I couldn't resist hugging her, no matter how unprofessional it was. I'd never been out East and I was dying to set foot in Manhattan.

"We're working two shows: Kourt Michaels Couture and Kimora's. It's going to be hard work Alex and these models will be a pain in the ass." She giggled, and continued, "But you'll love it!"

"This is my dream, and I won't let you down!"

I called Lilly as soon as I stepped into the hall outside of Lorena's office. "Guess who's on her way to New York City!"

~

Everything you hear about New York is true and then some. Of course, when you are in the fashion and beauty industry, you experience it from a whole different angle. I flew nonstop on Virgin America with four other makeup artists and stylists. We arrived at JFK just before eight that morning. Right away, I just knew I'd hate being in New York. I missed California already. By the time our van got to our Midtown hotel, I was ready to drop. Who can sleep on those red eye flights?

I rolled my sturdy hardware case inside the hotel while a bellman piled our personal bags onto the cart. I never parted with my makeup kit. When someone offered to help, I kindly refused. The contents alone were worth at least five thousand dollars. I learned early on to use only the best skincare and cosmetics; especially the brushes and applicators because those were what created the magic. My tools came from all over the world.

I didn't play around when it came to my work, and that meant I didn't play when it came to my money. My generous friends had no idea how much they helped kick start my career. Newcomers rarely come out the gate armed the way I did. You have to hustle, which is why I never turned down money. That was business. If you're going to take a man's money, make it work for you - for the long haul.

There was only time for a quick nap and maybe a bite to eat, before our group headed over to Bryant Park to check out the scene. I wore a navy blue Diane von Furstenberg dress, with brown suede Michael Kors knee boots and matching leather belted blazer. My hair was deeply curly because I let it air dry after showering. I felt freer in New York, so I kept it natural. A palm full of styling cream and I was ready to roll. I slung my Balenciaga over my shoulder and took off; outside to freeze my ass off, while trying to hail a taxi.

"You're never going to get anywhere like that!"

The honks and city noise were loud and irritating. I was still a bit jetlagged and the last thing I needed was some jerk trying to steal my taxi.

"Excuse me?"

I was not in the mood. I swung around in my frustration, only to find a man dressed in a long cashmere town coat over his finely tailored suit. He whistled and waved a taxi over.

He looked back at me with smile lines framing his beautiful teeth. "I thought I'd help you, is all. You're not from New York, are you?"

"Look, thank you. I'm just in a hurry; I really appreciate it, though!" I must have fumbled with my handbag just long enough.

"So am I. Would you like to share? I'm not a psycho, I promise." He chuckled as if he found it amusing to stand in thirty degree weather chatting about transportation.

I looked around and saw no other option. Someone had just jumped in the second taxi already. "Okay, I'm on my way to Bryant Park so I need to be the first stop." I was nodding to assure him there was to be no negotiating on that.

"Fantastic, let's go." He gestured for me to climb in. *Mmm… a gentleman.* After settling in, he removed his leather gloves while checking me out. "I'm Bryce."

I faintly shook his hand. "Alexia."

He nodded. "Welcome to New York, Alexia. Are you a model, or…?"

I laughed under my breath, looking out onto Fifth Avenue. "Nice one." Glancing down, I noticed his strong and manicured hands. I was distracted for a second. "Sorry. No, I'm a makeup artist and I'm here working the shows."

Of all the times for New York traffic to be a breeze, we arrived at the park in what seemed like just a few minutes.

"What a shame. This is your stop already." As we approached, Bryce handed me his card. "Call me before you leave the city. We can have coffee."

I took the card and read it. *Bryce Chase, CEO Chase Commodities.*

"Mr. Chase, tell me… why do you choose taxis over a limo?" I teased him, while really wanting to know.

"Now who's buying into the cliché?" He smiled, putting me at ease.

"Touché." We had arrived. "Well, this is me. Um…maybe I'll take you up on the coffee. I can't promise though, because it's a little crazy." I blindly reached into my bag for my own card. "Here! If you're ever in LA, call me. There's *lots* of coffee in LA." I winked at him and got out.

I met up with the team and we rushed inside the tents. The scene was pulsing with excitement. New York Fashion Week in all its glory. Yet, all I could think about at that moment was Mr. Chase and his Park Avenue smile.

Of course, I was just dying to know how he took his coffee.

The Power of Dowdy Wife

*T*he great thing about working in LA is you can play all day, party all night and still do a little business. Business and pleasure often overlap.

Stacee, a hot shot hairstylist I met with during the New York trip, and who I swear could be Nia Long's twin, had been invited to the premier of the latest action flick, starring Hayden Jones. Stacee has a reputation for being one of the best hairstylists in Los Angeles, and is known as the queen of the lace front wig. One of her VIP clients just happened to be the executive producer's wife.

A premier is not complete without hot parties to follow. In Hollywood, every social gathering is an opportunity. There's lots of potential at these soirées. You have to work the social scene if you want to make it big in a town like Los Angeles. Every contract, every job you land in film or TV is based on relationships. Your talent is secondary. That means lots of schmoozing, whether it sickens you or not.

Case in point – Stacee now has her own salon in a prime location in West Hollywood all because she was nice enough to take on a last minute client for the

American Music Awards a couple of seasons before. Stacee said she knew this client would be a piece of work. She talked the dowdy looking wife of a music executive into taking her under-kept dreadlocks down for the event. "We'll just polish it up a bit." That's what Stacee told her, while what she was really saying was when your husband is a major player you need to look a certain way.

Stacee's comment bothered me, just a little. As a young black girl whose mother is Bahamian, I grew up around dreads and other natural hairstyles. My hair was always curly and free, and it wasn't until my teen years that I began to blow-dry it while experimenting. Still, I had to fight the stereotypes. White people would say, 'Why don't you straighten your hair more often?' On the other hand black people told me to, 'Keep it natural.' I couldn't win. Now I do whatever I want. Even so, Stacee's comment reminded me of the bending we sometimes have to do to appease Hollywood. But, with all of that said, I admit **Dowdy Wife** benefited from the sprucing up.

When **Dowdy Wife** stepped out of the car that night, photographers were scrambling. They didn't recognize her. TMZ had to retract a story that Mr. Executive had brought his girlfriend to the awards show. The woman didn't look anything like her every day self. The attention given to **Dowdy Wife**, resulted in a boost in her self-confidence. The next thing you know Stacee was her regular stylist, with weekly appointments at **Dowdy Wife's** lavish Studio City home. That relationship evolved into friendship, and a major investment into Stacee's business plan - and Glam Lox was born.

You build and work every relationship until it takes a bad turn. Unfortunately, sometimes they do.

Attending a Hollywood event is not as simple as putting on lipstick and brushing your hair. You have to vamp it up. You never know who you'll meet, or rub elbows with, so to speak. And, because there are photographers everywhere, you have to be camera ready. If you're smart, you'll strike up a conversation with Mr. Magoo if you have to, because if he's the man of the hour, you want that photo op.

Still, Hollywood parties are a bore. With industry parties, you have to be ON at all times. There's no such thing as being you. Sometimes you have to sell out for what you want, and on this night I wanted to meet Hayden Jones.

Hayden was throwing one of his famous Hollywood parties after the premier. There was just one problem: I wasn't invited. But, I knew Stacee was, so I called her.

"Stacee, hey sweetie, how are you?"

I felt a little guilty because I really liked Stacee and this could have been mistaken as using her, but I needed in on that party. I had seen the girls Hayden was photographed with: the predictable Barbie dolls. He deserved better.

"Alex! What's up, girl?"

"Not too much. I'm supposed to go to a thing downtown, but I think not. I don't feel like dealing with…" I let my words trail off.

"Then you're coming with me, and don't say no!"

I wouldn't dare… "Why? Where are you headed tonight?"

"Hayden Jones is throwing a huge party at his house after the premier. I met him on the set a while back, when I was there with the producer's wife. He's good people. Do you know Hayden?"

Picking at my cuticle, hiding the fact that I was dying to meet him, I paused for a second. "No, but I hear he's a sweetheart. Are you sure you can bring a friend?"

"He is…and please, he will not mind - trust me. Go to your party if you want, but be back at your place by eleven. I'll pick you up shortly after. Kisses!"

Swoosh! I'd heard tale of Hayden Jones and was curious to find out if it were all true. I wanted to know what his story was, and knew this was my one shot at finding out.

Nothing was going to stop me.

An eerie decadence

*T*he first thing I saw as we drove up to Hayden's contemporary Kimridge Road home in Beverly Hills that March night, were leggy, wannabe starlets in mini dresses, stilettos and pageant hair. I expected a more polished crowd. They were standing at the gate primping and fluffing each other's hair like they were about to audition for a music video.

I admit to being surprised to find that Hayden lived in such a calm residential neighborhood. I would have thought an ocean front party palace in Malibu was more his style; the typical panty trap. Not Hayden. Though he had a well earned lover boy reputation, he made it crystal clear that he was not just another highly paid flash in the pan actor, seeking publicity. He was an A-list movie star; hence the girls clawing at the bricks and using their huge boobs to work past the gate. Like me, they had all heard the stories. Hayden treated his girlfriends very well. Notice I used plural.

You could see the house from the street, with its glass walls and dimmed interior. Beyond the iron gates, hedges and flickers of light reflecting from a water fixture in the circular drive, was music and hedonistic laughter coming from the rear of the property. It was seductive and I couldn't wait to get inside. If I got Hayden to notice me just for a few minutes, and lure him away from the harem at the gates, maybe we could actually engage in nice conversation.

When we stopped at the Valet stand, I climbed out of Stacee's Lexus and adjusted the belt of my strapless Tracy Reese jumpsuit. I silently thanked God I hadn't worn some mini dress because I wanted to stand out and not look too typical.

"What is this, a groupie-thon?" Stacee rolled her eyes and tucked her clutch under her arm, handing the valet her keys.

I admired how Stacee's petite and curvy body worked the Herve Leger bandage dress. There was an inherent sexiness to her that drew men like bees to honey.

"I know damn well Hayden Jones can pull a better grade than this." She scrunched her face, laughing under her breath.

I giggled and glanced at the hopefuls who were now tossing low-brow glares at us. "Oh, I'm sure he can."

It was pretty dark with the exception of the gas lanterns at the gate and low beam lights from the security van. Stacee waved her invitation at the bulky, but cute guy, as we kept through the side gate he was manning. Through the glass doors at the entrance of the house, I could see figures milling around inside. Dance music pumped from around the rear. The whole scene gave off a kind of eerie decadence.

"Ladies, come with me!"

Out of nowhere, a guy in his early twenties, who was skinny, extremely pale with flaming red cropped hair and assumedly gay, grabbed both of our hands and guided us inside the house.

"Where are we going?"

I couldn't help but laugh because it was so strange. He focused straight ahead, with a smirk on his face. This guy reminded me of a younger David Caruso; only a lot prettier.

"After you…Hurry, before the trash follows us." Our escort extended his arm and winked at Stacee, as we went in.

Stacee gave him a glance over. "Thank you. By the way, you are…?" She was more suspicious than I, who at this point was as curious as Alice in an adult Wonderland.

"You two looked misplaced wandering around out there. I saved you." Pretty Caruso waved over a staffer carrying a tray of wine. "Drinks for my girls, please." He handed me a glass. "I'm Kaz, Hayden's assistant."

Pretty Caruso had my absolute attention.

"It's nice to meet you, Kaz. I'm Alex."

It was then that I noticed the music was more laid back inside of the house. Sting's vocals echoed off the walls.

"Likewise..." He took another glass from the tray and handed it to Stacee. "...for you."

"Aw, thank you, I'm Stacee." She raised her brows at me and her eyes smiled as she sipped the smooth vino.

Surveying the two story entrance, I admired the space and watched party goers huddled in groups laughing and drinking. The inside crowd was definitely more sophisticated. Wondering where our host might be, I chattered away, keeping Kaz right by our side. "Nice party..." I nodded, enjoying my drink.

"It is in here." Kaz went on about how Hayden threw these parties and didn't really mingle with most of his guests. Saying it was an entirely different experience if you were lucky enough to be invited inside of his house. "This is why I rescued you two from being swallowed up by the wannabes outside." He waved at someone coming through the door. "Give me a minute, will you? Enjoy yourselves." Pretty Caruso sashayed away in his white skinny jeans.

"Alex, I'm going to check out the scene a bit. I think I

see somebody I know."

What was I supposed to do now?

Stacee disappeared through the doors leading outside to the patio and pool. Some platinum blonde in electric blue metallic jeans and who looked strangely familiar sat at the foot of the staircase texting in her phone. When her friend walked up to her, and she cracked up laughing, I recognized the girl from a popular network drama. It was all so surreal. I suddenly felt self conscious, so I played it cool and wandered into the living room, admiring the wall art. Surely Stacee or Pretty Caruso would be back in a minute, I thought.

"This poor guy got ripped off on that one. What do you think?"

The voice behind me was cocky and I felt a need to defend our host's choice. *Who the hell asked you?* I thought.

"Are you serious? I love it. I mean, I don't know what it cost, but there's something about her eyes. They're..." I turned around to continue my inexperienced appraisal of expensive watercolors.

His smile floored me.

Hayden stood there staring at me, and I was speechless. My feet went numb. Let's face it, he wasn't just *some* guy. He was the onscreen hero, the cute boyfriend in the occasional romantic comedy and Hollywood's infamous charmer. Those evident facial features (the kissable lips, dimples and the chestnut eyes) that the world fell in love with on screen were a softer version in person. He wasn't just handsome, Hayden was beautiful. Even People magazine said so. I felt so tiny standing next to him. My five-foot-three self, compared to his six-two stature. Surprisingly though, I wasn't intimidated. My just-say-no response had already been dialed up in my head. It was the only way to spare myself.

"…her eyes are sad." Clearing my throat I struggled to compose myself.

Hayden had his arms folded behind him. "She's not sad. She just doesn't know where she fits in, that's all." He shifted his eyes from mine and back to the painting. Was he describing the girl in the painting, or me?

Hayden focused on it as if it were the first time he'd seen the portrait. The spotlight softly shone onto his eyes. I wanted to touch his face, that jaw line and where his dimples sank in when he smiled minutely.

"Maybe, I…I don't know." I fiddled with my purse. "You have a beautiful home. I'm here with my friend." I peered past Hayden, pretending to look for Stacee. "I'm not sure where she went."

Hayden bit his bottom lip, trying not to smile as he

could sense I was nervous. "Well, thank you, and I'm sure she'll make it back." He extended his hand. "I'm Hayden."

"Sorry, I'm Alexia. But, you can call me Alex."

"Alexia..." He took the time to pronounce every syllable of my name. "It's a beautiful name and I can't imagine shortening it."

There it started; the seduction. But who was seducing whom?

Hayden and I talked for around two hours that night. Stacee, strutting back in smelling like weed, found us in the kitchen sitting at the counter. It was well after two in the morning and I didn't want to leave but knew I should, or I'd be a goner.

"Miss Stacee James... Wearing that dress like you mean it!" Hayden teased as he stood and hugged Stacee.

"Baby boy, I always mean it... Hi, handsome." She looked at the both of us, slyly. "What are ya'll up to, hiding in here?" Stacee emptied the bottle of Veuve Clicquot into a glass.

Hayden handed her a bowl of strawberries. "So did you enjoy it?" He waited for Stacee's critique. "It's just us here, so tell the truth."

Stacee popped a strawberry in her mouth, holding up a finger. "Mmm, good....yes, I did. You were a little crazy though. I mean, your character was, you know…"

"No, you're right. He's a complete sociopath." Hayden talked with Stacee about the film while his eyes locked into mine.

He made me so uneasy. I usually didn't let men do that to me. But Hayden – he caught me off guard and I hated it. The plan was to go there and wrap Hayden Jones around my finger. Just to see what would happen.

"Hayden, thank you for having us and congratulations on the film. It's going to do great, I know it." Stacee took off looking for the bathroom or something.

"I appreciate that, Stacee."

I gathered my things and stalled, blindly fumbling my hand around in my handbag. At that moment I didn't need to be left alone with Hayden. He was the type of guy I could really like. It's as if because he wasn't trying to impress me, I didn't know how to react, or what to say.

"Okay, well…I'm going to go find Stacee, it's getting late and I have an appointment in the morning." I lied.

Hayden walked me to the front of the house and then Pretty Caruso reappeared out of the blue.

"What's going on, guys? Oh, Hayden… the house is cleared. Some of my friends are still here, but we're on our way to an after-hours thing." Pretty Caruso grinned at me. "I see you've met my new friend, Alex." Rambling like he was on speed, he kept talking, "Okay - I'll be by tomorrow afternoon." And like that, he was gone again.

"I wish I had his energy." I laughed.

"Yeah, he's uh, definitely hyper; but a solid guy. He's takes care of everything for me."

"Everything?" I teased, trying to ease the awkwardness.

"Sure, like tonight. Just when I was ready to kick everyone out, he found you."

All I could do was avert my eyes to his beautiful neck, underneath the black V-neck tee he wore. *Say something and don't sound stupid.* "Hey well, there you go. Alex saves the day."

"Alexia…" He reached over and slid my phone out of my hand and typed into it. "…maybe we can hang out sometime… whatever you want. The second number is mine; the first is Kaz's. He can reach me anywhere." Hayden was a little presumptuous, but I enjoyed that about him.

"That would be fun." My hand was trembling and I hoped he hadn't noticed. *Why did he give me his number?* Now I had to decide if and when I'd call him. It's not like he would be sitting around waiting for my call.

We exchanged a friendly hug, during which I slyly rubbed my fingers across the nape of his neck, grazing his cropped wavy hair. It was time to get out of there. I briskly walked out past the fountain and out the gate. Stacee was waiting in her car. There were only a few others still out front.

"What happened back there, girl?"

"I don't know, but I think Hayden just asked me out. Sort of…" Puzzled, I looked at Stacee and waited for her to burst my bubble. Instead she just smiled.

The drive back to my place was quiet. Stacee was probably tipsy and I was still under some kind of spell. I wanted to call Lilly and get her thoughts. It seemed silly. Still, I needed her take on it. Run down the entire evening. I decided not to.

All night I fought the notion that Hayden was just being nice and that I'd never hear from him again.

I needed to curtail those feelings. I decided I'd call Erik for coffee the next morning.

Grow up!

It was now mid April and Erik called out of the blue wanting to meet up again. I hadn't seen him in almost a month, around the time of Hayden's party. We made plans for lunch at The Peninsula's roof garden restaurant.

When I got there just after one o'clock, he was already seated in one of the tucked away corners of the terrace.

"In spite of what you think, I don't enjoy the Hollywood crowd much." Erik pulled his sunglasses off and cradled them at the opening of his shirt.

I could tell something was off about Erik. He wasn't his usual cool self. One of the things I enjoyed about him was his innate ability to make me feel at ease because he knew how to handle anything and anyone. Not this day. He was jittery.

"Erik, you okay?" I looked through the menu.

"Of course, I'm fine. I've just got so much bloody nonsense to work out before I leave for New York. I told you I'm going to New York, right?" He hadn't and I think he knew it. Not that he had to.

"No, but that's good… right? Your mother will be pleased to have you home." I smiled, trying to assure him of that.

"I said I'm going to New York, not Long Island. The North Shore hardly qualifies as New York!" Erik was belligerent; hostile, even.

"Whatever…" I wished I hadn't come.

The server came over and I ordered a chef salad and a glass of orange juice. Erik was drowning in coffee.

"Yeah – so anyway, it's just for a couple of weeks."

"Erik, you look awful. What's going on?" I was concerned.

"Nothing, I just wanted to see you." He poured more sugar into the cup. "You're my friend, right?"

"You know I am." Watching his every gesture, I wondered why his hands were shaking.

"I can't be in LA right now. It's like a cesspool. Bloodsucking leaches!" Erik made no sense at all.

"What are you talking about?" I looked him over, trying to imagine what the real issue might be.

"I just wanted to see you before I leave tonight. I'll be staying at the Waldorf Towers. I need to clear my head and I can't do it here." As evasive as he was, I almost felt as if he was begging me to talk him out of leaving.

"Erik, listen… I don't know what's going on, but I want to remind you of something. You're the one who told me to always look out for myself. Now I'm telling you. Whatever reason you have, if you're running away for a minute or whatever…take care of yourself."

The conversation was completely draining and I needed a drink, but decided not to have one. My salad came and I picked over it.

"Alex, this is why I called you. You're the only girl I know right now who isn't completely selfish."

"Hmmm, I don't know. You're giving me too much credit, Erik." I laughed under my breath looking up at him, though there was nothing funny about the moment.

I didn't try to talk Erik out of leaving, because I was *sure* he was avoiding something.

A couple of days later I found out that he had been slapped with a paternity suit. Lilly called me with the news.

"Alex, can you believe Erik is denying it? Just pay the girl and be done, you know?"

"Pay and be done? Lilly, how about grow up and be a father instead of a sperm donor?"

"Erik doesn't know how to be a father. He's a spoiled brat. You know that."

She was right. Erik was spoiled, entitled and didn't know how to take care of anyone but himself. Sure, eventually he paid a hefty sum to the mother. He even came back to Los Angeles, pretending to be with her as they paraded around town like a budding couple. Soon enough though, he got bored and broke it off. *Chandler Mahron's brother dumps pregnant girlfriend weeks before the birth* is how the gossip columns described it. I realized there are always two sides to a story, but this version sounded about right.

No matter which was true, I chose to no longer have any part of it.

That was the last time I saw Erik Mahron.

Lookie-loo, you see that?

was sick as a dog. My insides were tight, like I could vomit at any moment. I had never felt like that before, or since and only had myself and that bottle of wine to blame.

All I could do was curl up in my chair and gaze out the window. No matter how gross I felt, I basked in that there was possibly a new man in my life. How it would end, only God knew. But, at that moment, I didn't even care about the details.

~

Do you remember Mr. Manhattan taxi, Bryce Chase? Well, he finally called. I had actually forgotten about him. There was a dinner party being thrown in his honor at his friend, media heiress and socialite Melania Blakemore's estate in Holmby Hills. Bryce was so gentlemanly that he came for me in a limousine. It was almost like a date, though he didn't push me.

"So what will your friend think of you bringing another woman to dinner?" I asked, bracing myself for what I was getting myself into.

"It's not like that. Melania is the widow of one of my dearest friends. I visit her and the children now and then. They're like family. When I was married, we were all best friends. I made a promise, you know?"

I understood. There was nothing more to say. I wanted to be respectful of the situation and appreciated that Bryce gave me the lowdown before we got there.

Melania was absolutely gracious. Immediately she told me, "If you are a friend of Bryce's, I welcome you into my home, Alexia." She greeted me with a double kisses and a waltz through her home in the most beautiful Givenchy gown I'd seen since Fashion Week. She cupped my hands and paid me a compliment. "I have this gown in red, but Ralph Lauren was made for you. It doesn't look like this on me, my dear." I doubted that, but appreciated how kind she was.

After dinner Bryce took me for drinks at the Bar at The Peninsula. It was a Wednesday night just before ten. The interesting thing is that out-of-towners think that Saturday is the night to see and be seen. But, what they don't know is that when you're in Beverly Hills or Hollywood, every night is the night to be seen. Typically, the wealthy and famous hide out on the weekends. They stay behind closed doors of their posh estates or secret locations that are off limits to the average Joe. Weekends are when tourists are on the prowl with their digitals and camera phones taking photos of the famous faces, to share with their friends.

The Bar was dark and romantic, as usual.

"Good evening Sir, and welcome back." The bartender greeted us as Bryce guided me to a cozy section across from the bar. There was soft music playing and the mood was the perfect ending to a relaxed evening.

"Are you a regular, Bryce?"

He loosened his tie, "Actually, I had dinner in the restaurant last night and well...they remember me, I suppose."

"Of course they do." I glanced up and gave a friendly smile to the bartender in his crisp white jacket. He was really cute; probably an actor, I thought. "Are you staying here in the hotel? I assumed you were a guess of Miss Blakemore's."

"No, I don't stay there. It would be too confusing for the children." Bryce answered quickly and looked uncomfortable speaking on the topic.

If there was some type of drama going on, I hoped I could end the night without being brought into another man's sad episode.

"Understandable."

I excused myself to the ladies room, recalling how mysterious Bryce seemed in New York, and that I couldn't wait to share coffee with him. During that short walk across the lobby, it occurred to me that we didn't have anything in common. Bryce was nice company, but I wasn't keen on getting to know him much further than that. I just wanted to finish up the evening and call it. I hoped he didn't throw a wrench in the plan and invite me to his suite, because I'd have to come up with a sharp excuse or cave in and feel like a fool in the morning.

"Hurry up, they're waiting!" A woman's husky voice echoed out of a stall next to mine. Craning my neck so that I could hear a little better, I heard more than I cared to. "Shhh! Dammit, don't drop it." Long, loud snorts followed.

I heard more sets of heels stomping into the ladies lounge. Whoever it was didn't come into the stalls area. I hurried to get out of there because I didn't want to witness anything too crazy.

As I entered the lounge area, two girls in sparkling tops, tight skirts and cheap shoes, with cameras dangling from their wrists, stood at the vanities. One of them looked up at my reflection in the mirror and the other flung her head around. I nodded and washed my hands, then refreshed my lipstick. It was obvious they were hoping to catch a glimpse of someone rich and famous. The disappointment filled their eyes when it was just me.

That disappointment would be short lived, because crime drama actress and cosmetics spokesmodel Faye Nichols came stumbling out of a stall with a nameless friend.

"Hi there, ladies." Faye didn't have enough sense to get out there.

The wide-eyed hopefuls from Middle America slapped each other's arms when they recognized her. One of the girls snapped a photo on the low. As I pretended to swipe more lip color on, I watched her hands hold the camera at waist level and aim upward to get a shot, while Faye wiped a white powdery residue from her flaming red nostril. What a dummy.

I thought *Lookie-loo, did you see that?* I don't know if those girls knew what was going down, but I wondered how long it would take for the image of the coked up, oblivious actress to end up on the internet or worse. I shook my head, laughing at the whole pathetic scene and walked out.

When I got back to Bryce there was a bottle of champagne waiting. And, so was a skinny brunette who was sitting in one of the club chairs next to mine. She had made herself at home, tottering at the edge of the chair, with her legs crossed. Engrossed in chatter, she fanned her crimson tipped claws in the air.

"Alexia, good you're back!" *Right...* I thought. Bryce stood, as did the girl. "I'd like you to meet a dear friend of mine."

I realized then that Mr. Manhattan had quite a few dear friends around town. The girl had this *I've got him, honey* expression on her face. "I'm Deidra. It's a pleasure, Alexia." I could see the wheels spinning in that brain of hers as she tried to figure out why I was so cool.

Bryce hadn't bothered with formal introductions. At the moment though, I was just simply relieved that he had given me an out. The night was going nowhere.

I nodded. "Deidra..." The girl took a step away, but I stopped her. "Oh...you don't have to leave." While I was enjoying the puzzled look on Bryce's face, my phone vibrated from inside of my evening bag. *Saved by the bell.* "Bryce, you've been a sweetheart, but this headache will not let up, and I'm feeling dizzy. You don't want to deal with this, trust me."

Bryce sipped his champagne, and grinned at me. All I could do was give him a hug and say goodnight. I whispered in his ear, "She'll take care of you, I'm sure. We'll talk soon."

His only comeback was, "I understand."

There was nothing more to say. Mr. Manhattan knew he was caught in a jam and that I was letting him off the hook. I couldn't have cared less really.

"Goodnight, you two."

Just as I climbed into the limo my phone buzzed again. (That's right – the limo stayed with me.) I didn't recognize the number, but I dialed back while glancing out at the row of luxury cars and the sparkling fountain as we exited onto Santa Monica Boulevard. "Hello? Someone called this number?"

"Alexia?"

I couldn't place the vaguely familiar voice. "Yes?"

"Hi, I'm glad you called back. It's Hayden."

Bryce was kicked from my memory just like that. I sat speechless for a few seconds, grinning like the Cheshire Cat. "Hi… What a nice surprise. How are you?" I ran my fingers through my hair, as if he was watching.

"I'm good. In fact, I'm on location in Vancouver, but thought of you today and wondered…why hasn't she called me?" He had the most adorable soft, sexy laugh.

I giggled, "Right, I'm sure you're sooo heartbroken."

Hayden gave me butterflies. I was blushing like crazy, but also hoping the conversation would be brief because I didn't want to appear afraid to talk to him. It wasn't a star struck emotion or anything. I was truly happy to hear his voice. Gazing past the driver and out the front window, that night we met flashed before my eyes. It had been a month, but I still remembered the details clearly.

"No...just a little dejected maybe." I could almost hear his smile. "Actually, it gets crazy and before I know it I've missed everything that's really important; like having a life."

"I can imagine. So how long will you be in Canada?" Fidgeting with my seatbelt buckle, I wanted to ask about the movie, what it's about, who's in it, etc... but I didn't dare.

"I'll be back in LA on Monday night." He sighed, "Then I come back to Vancouver in two weeks. There have been delays in shooting some final scenes, so..." There was a knock in the background. "I'll be out in a minute! - Alexia, I'm sorry..."

"It's okay. Hayden, I want to thank you again for a great time that night."

"I'm glad you were there." He paused. "You want to have dinner when I get back? We need to finish our conversation."

During a long silence, I pretended to think about his suggestion. "Sounds great, just let me know. Call me when you're back in town – anytime." I wished I hadn't thrown in that last part: *Anytime.* Hoping I didn't seem too giddy.

"I will. Have a good night, Alexia." I loved the way

he insisted on my proper name. Hayden knew how to make me feel special. From the very beginning.

"Thank you. Goodnight, Hayden."

I sat staring at my cell phone as if his face would appear. It was amazing what had just happened. Fresh off one of the most meaningless nights ever, came the best feeling I'd had in a long time; while hoping I wasn't setting myself up for disappointment.

When I got into my apartment, I fell across my fluffy couch and hugged a pillow wondering what was about to happen. Whatever would be, I knew Hayden Jones would be my ultimate experience. I could feel it.

So flighty over possibly being on his mind at that very moment, I decided to celebrate. I popped the cork of my favorite Merlot while Eric Benet sang out from the stereo. A while later, I woke up curled in a chair in the corner of the room, watching the taillights cruise down Rossmore Avenue. Gazing at the half empty bottle of wine on my coffee table, my feet felt light as they dangled over the arm of the chair. Finally making it to my room I crawled into bed.

Even though the wine had made me a little sick, it was the best night sleep I'd had in ages. You know the kind peace you have when there's every reason to be hopeful about entering into fresh romantic territory.

Not sure where it would lead, I was glad that Hayden called me first. It sounds silly, but that factor is important to most women. I thanked God a million times I hadn't humiliated myself and called him. Just because he offered his number, doesn't mean I had to or should initiate the chase. If I had - to this day I would have wondered if Hayden really wanted me, or was being generous. My judgment had worked for me so far.

Something I would fail at later.

Your smile's my favorite part

$\mathcal{H}$ayden knew what he wanted and unbeknownst to me, he had decided I was meant for him. I became seduced by his life and couldn't get enough. Lilly and I hadn't been hanging out as much. I wanted to tell her what was happening, but didn't want to jinx it so to speak. She picked up on it, though.

"What's going on, Alex? You've been acting so mysterious."

Of course I answered her with a question and tried to play light of it saying I was just working hard and seeing some guy, nothing big...all of that. I kept Hayden a secret, because he made me feel amazing and I wanted him all to myself, just for a little while. Once people found out, that feeling could be over.

In early June, I cancelled a commercial job in New York because Hayden was taking me to Hawaii.

How did this all happen, you ask?

Hayden had just gotten back in town, and he invited me to have dinner at his place. He didn't send a car for me or anything like that. He showed up at my door a few minutes before I was about to drive to his house. He told me he had never really had the chance to date anyone. With him it was always choice-pick with women; groupies and starlets alike, I'm sure. I was surprised to have him come fetch me, if you will. It was kind of old fashioned and I love it.

"I hope you don't mind. I felt like…" Still standing in the doorway, he brushed a strand of hair away from my face. "…I wanted to come and get you."

He was wearing jeans and a light blue unbuttoned shirt, which was wasn't tucked, with the sleeves rolled. He was so sexy standing there, and I admit, I couldn't help slyly checking out the blue faced Rolex Submariner on his wrist.

"Oh, of course not…come in. I'm glad you did."

I had on khaki dress shorts and a floral off the shoulder gypsy style blouse and Tory Burch sandals. I wanted to be cute without giving him too much. Hayden made himself at home while I went to get my handbag. When I got back into the living room, I found him flipping through some old books on the shelf.

"I'm a collector and I love the smell of worn, ragged books. Downloading books is not for me, you know?" Books were something that was my thing and not many guys I dated shared that interest.

"Me neither. I'm pretty old school." He smiled, giving me the once-over which made me a little self conscious. It seemed so surreal having Hayden Jones in my living room. No one would have believed how *real* he was.

"Nice. We're off to a good start then." I giggled. "Well, if you're ready..."

Somehow Hayden had found a parking spot for his shiny black Range Rover right in front of my building. Rossmore is busy and that fortune never happens to visitors. It was like the magic of celebrity. I usually parked my car in the garage, but even if I wanted, I could never find a spot out front - and I lived there. I suppose had I upgraded from a Jetta to some hundred-thousand-dollar ride, maybe I could have.

In reality's light Hayden was pretty normal. It was just me with a new guy. That notion was kicked out when we made stops along the way. Like at the wine shop on Canon Drive. Two busty girls nearly knocked over the displays because they were bubbling with excitement over the presence of my "normal" guy. He had sunglasses on and tried to pretend he hadn't noticed them. But, I know he enjoyed it.

Checking out the selection and reading various labels, he decided, "We need an after dinner wine as well, so pick one. Whatever you like!" Hayden peered over the top of his sunglasses and chuckled at my bewilderment. Like he assumed I wouldn't want to choose for him.

I flung my bag on my shoulder. "Alright, putting me on the spot, huh? I know *exactly* which one. You'll love it, because I do." I glanced behind him and caught this fifty-something lady eavesdropping and I wished she'd walk away. Hayden must have sensed my discomfort. I picked up the Moscato and pretended to examine the label.

He folded his arms, turning around to the lady, "See – this is the test. If she doesn't know a good wine, how can I possibly marry her?"

The woman's jaw dropped and her eyes were as big as saucers.

Quickly looking up at him, my brows scrunched and I blushed uncontrollably. "Stop that!" As if I needed to, I mouthed to the woman, *He's kidding.* Hayden was disarming my independence. I didn't like it.

"Alright, if you say so." He grinned and took the bottles from my hands, walking towards the cashier.

Just then a man dressed in an outdated golf outfit walked in the shop and recognized Hayden. He shook his hand and asked for a photo, which Hayden obliged. All I could do was watch and soak it in. I was still stuck on Hayden's jesting words to the woman, but it was playful and lightened the mood. I basked in the company of my movie star date.

Hayden cooked dinner for me. Under the watchful eye of a hired chef, that is. Then we ate outside on the terrace. It was a cool night, so we lit the fire pit, and after dinner snuggled under a blanket. It couldn't have been more perfect.

I learned a lot about Hayden that night. Like the fact that he was thirty-four years old, got his first acting gig at eleven years old starring in a cereal commercial, and had what he described as a culturally challenging childhood, being that his dad was black and his mom is Jewish. His dad had died some years before. To my surprise, Hayden also talked about being married and divorced by the time he was twenty-five. I was glad that I had never known that about him, so my response was sincere. We swapped stories about our families and the big dreams we had as kids; essentially how we both ended up in Los Angeles.

"Thank you for being here, Alex." He sipped his wine, wiping a little from his lips while gazing into my eyes like he was searching for soul secrets.

"Finally, you call me Alex!" I giggled rubbing my hand along his firm arm. I could feel my cheeks become flushed as I averted my eyes to the dancing flames of the stone pit.

"You're beautiful… and your smile is my favorite part."

Just like that - as corny as that sounds, I fell head first.

It was late when I remembered I hadn't driven. I offered to take a cab home but Hayden wouldn't have it and insisted I stay in one of the guest rooms, which he showed me to himself.

On his way out of the room he hugged me. A cradling and strong, wrap-around hug and it felt so comfortable to be in his arms. It had been a long time since I'd felt that way. He looked into my eyes for a few seconds, held my face and kissed me. His soft lips kissed the side of my mouth, the tip of my nose and then my lips. My mind was all over the map. I wondered *is this how he kisses his leading ladies…and his girlfriends?* All of those slutty looking girls clamoring around at the party crossed my mind. Just as quickly though, I dismissed those visuals. Hayden could have hooked up with any one of them, but he chose to spend time with me that night. At that, I held the back of his neck with my hand and encouraged a deeper kiss. Then he stopped, giving me another quick peck before backing away.

I was so confused.

"Make yourself at home. Sleep well and for as late as you want, alright?"

He flashed that famous dimpled grin, pulled the door closed and that was it. I was a little surprised that Hayden never came back knocking on the door for a little nightcap. Pleasantly surprised I might add, because the chemistry between us was undeniable, but he was a gentleman about it. I wondered how long that would last.

It was too good to be true; Hayden's determination for me to trust him. I looked forward to everything that would come next. As long as it included him, I foolishly didn't care which direction things went.

In the morning, I met Miss Sylvie.

Her voice awakened me from sleep.

"Good morning…"

She brought me breakfast, and tossed what *I felt* was a judgmental glance as I pulled the covers to my naked chest. I was so embarrassed.

"Good morning. Um…is Hayden still here?"

She wasn't fazed by seeing a naked girl in the guestroom. I was sure this woman had witnessed lots of curious events in that house.

"Yes, he's in the gym, but said you might be hungry. He'll be done soon." I sat up, reaching for my blouse, watching her place the tray on the bench at the foot of the bed. Something about this woman felt close to home.

Not just that she was black, but she was nurturing and soft spoken, yet had that assured tone to her accent; like my mother. "I didn't know what you'd like ma'am, so whatever...is all here."

"Thank you." I ogled over the tempting presentation of waffles, strawberries and other assorted fruits, juices and water. I tried engaging in small talk to ease the awkwardness. "If I may ask, you're not from Los Angeles, are you?"

"No, no...Freeport..." She didn't look up as she kept attending to the food. I cut her off.

"Bahamas? Of course...I knew it. My mother's people are from Eleuthera. Most are still there."

"You don't say." She glanced up at me with a smile creeping to her eyes. "Well, enjoy your breakfast, dear."

I couldn't have eaten it all, but I tried. Attempting to appear modest, I reached for a kiwi first. "I'm Alex, by the way... and, thank you for breakfast."

She poured some orange juice for me. "I'm Sylvie, and it is my pleasure. There are plenty of towels in the bath." She gave me a pat on the arm, smiled and left.

How did Sylvie end up taking care of Hayden? It's like she was his second mother. If that entire overnighter was some staged attempt to woo me, it worked. I didn't want to leave, and felt like I belonged there.

Hayden and I saw each other quite a bit over the next

couple of weeks, before he went back to Canada. As independent as I was, my own projects began to feel like fillers until he got back to town.

That was the beginning of it all.

And - that's where Hawaii comes in.

Celebrity changes the game

"We've wrapped and I'm leaving for Maui in a week."

"For how long?" I lay in my bed and held that phone to my ear for what seemed like minutes waiting for Hayden to respond.

"I don't know. How long can you be gone for?"

Is he serious? "What are you saying?"

"Come with me."

Why'd he throw that unfair invite at me? I knew it wasn't smart to go away with him on a whim like that. I had landed a big gig in New York and would be paid well for it. "Hayden, I don't know…"

"Okay look, I have a house there and I just want you to experience the *real* Hawaii and for us to spend some time with away from LA. You'll have your own space, I promise. Please, say you'll come."

He poured on all of the persuasion, encouraging my decision; while at the same time it was clear that whether or not I went, he was leaving for paradise. I tried my strongest to push back all those weeks before, but the truth of the matter was… I had fallen in love. That meant I feared what his being in Hawaii without me might turn into, so I caved in.

I took a big swallow of wine, "So - when do we leave?" I gleefully accepted the chance to spend some hot romance time with him away from the glare of Hollywood eyes. All the while, knowing it was bound to be a mistake.

"Really?" There was surprise in his voice. "You're going to have an unforgettable time Alex, I promise."

I was sure of that, but was a little scared as well. Hayden is famous and when you date a famous man, people make assumptions about you. The type of assumptions I wasn't ready to take on.

This kind of celebrity changes the game. You have the assistants, managers, family and friends, even fans who buck against the relationship. Up until that point, Hayden and I had been seeing each other under the radar, but once we hit Hawaii, that would be over. I chose to hold on to it for as long as possible. I didn't tell Lilly a thing before we left. Once, I mentioned that I met Hayden Jones at a party. That's it. But, about Hawaii, I lied and said that Lorena invited some of us to her house in Maui. She seemed to have bought it. Lilly was easily excited and would have leaked it all to the tabloids herself out of sheer joy.

Tree house on the hill

$\mathcal{I}$f anyone had thought Hayden was just a pretty boy who couldn't take care of himself, they would have assumed wrong.

There was no staff waiting on us, and Hayden himself woke up and had breakfast ready by nine, every day. We cooked dinner together in the evenings; without a chef. Sure, the cleaning lady came in while we were out during the day, but all in all... we had the house to ourselves. In that week of bliss, we swam, hiked and biked through the mountains. I took board lessons while Hayden actually surfed. I don't know, but I expected him to show off and try to impress me the way Erik and all the other men I'd met did. But, that's what I loved about Hayden, the fact that he didn't try too hard.

The man turned me on just by breathing and that's not even the sex talking. He was actually fun. Hayden *lived* life and didn't just flaunt his money. He brought out interests in me that I never knew I had.

For instance, I never thought I'd enjoy a week in the mountains. Hayden's house was on a hilltop of Wailuku. We drove for what seemed like forever on a winding road, before finally passing through the entrance, on the palm lined path to paradise.

"I spent a lot of time here growing up, Alex. We're almost at the house." Hayden was at home in Hawaii and I cherished being there with him.

"It's amazing up here." I was trying not to be in awe, but when we walked inside and I looked around the vast room and then ahead through the windows before me, I couldn't pretend. It was like we were floating above the trees.

"Hayden, it's like a tree house!"

"It's great, isn't it? Wait until you see the rest."

A luxurious, two-thousand square foot, mountain top tree house, mind you. Complete with a wraparound porch amidst exotic plants and flowers, palm trees, with perimeter views of the ocean. How was I supposed to not fall head over hills for him in that setting? I wanted so badly to tell Hayden I loved him - but fought it.

I saw a more relaxed side of Hayden in Maui. We shared a lot with each other. I'm surprised that I trusted him enough to open up as much as I did. But, the conversation after dinner the first night changed the tone of our friendship.

"This is the first time I've brought anyone here; to this house, I mean." Hayden sipped from the longneck bottle as he leaned back in one of the Adirondack chairs and stared out over the rail into the darkness. The moon reflecting off the water at the bottom of the hill created a melancholy moment and I guess confessions were in order. "My parents first brought me to this town as a kid and it's the only place I can be myself."

Hearing him say those words made me realize the burden he carried and how it must feel to be someone else all the time. "Then, I can't tell you how glad I am that you invited me."

He turned to me, "It's *why* I invited you." He gestured, "Come sit with me." Hayden clutched my hand guiding me out of my own chair. I lay back against him; his arms enveloping me.

I wasn't sure if he was being honest about me being the first girl invited there, but I loved that he told me that. He allowed his vulnerability to show and the men I'd been with before him, kept up a callused appearance. Playing the hard role, they never let me in, but Hayden did. In turn, I began to trust that his feelings towards me were real.

Hayden and I managed to keep the first couple of days to ourselves. No one knew where we were. That is except for his manager Rusty Fisk who seemed to check in every other hour; as if Hayden had run off and was never returning to LA. Finally, he tossed me his phone and said, "Tell Rusty I'm not in and to stop calling!" He

laughed, but with a serious look on his face. "Go on, tell
him." Instead, I walked over to the sofa where Hayden
was lying and curled up to him with good ol' Rusty on
speakerphone, ranting and talking to the wind. I finally
just turned off the power.

Hawaii was the first time we slept together. In all the
romantic build-up, I didn't know what to expect.
Hayden held back all those weeks leading up (I'm still
pretty sure one of his adoring stowaways took care of
him while he perched me on the pedestal of virtue) But,
on that first night – Hayden made love to me like I was
the only woman in the world he had *ever* wanted. It was
so intense that it scared me at first, but then I decided I
deserved what he was giving me - his soul. When it
came to relationships I was usually the one who fell
hard, but Hayden knew what he wanted and pounced
on it. He had a plan, and it included me.

On the last night at the house, we went walking on
the beach.

Hayden asked me to marry him.

He flung a rock into the ocean and blurted, "Marry
me!" I thought he was crazy.

I grabbed his arm. "Hayden you're not serious. We
haven't known each other long enough. You can't be…"

"Would it be better if we waited another couple of

months?" I knew right then, he was completely serious. "I spent a year convincing myself that I loved someone once, and then married her only to find out it was completely wrong. She didn't give a damn about me."

I had never met anyone who made me feel as loved and safe as Hayden did. Because of that, I had so much love for him in my heart. I wanted to spend every minute I could with him. But, marriage?

"That's not who I am and I think you know that. I might even be in love with you, but I'm struggling with it because...well, what makes you so sure about this? You have to let me know you're for real."

"When you showed up at my house that night, it was like we'd known each other for years. Alexia, I love you and I want you in my life every day. I don't need more time to know that. So, let's take a chance." He smiled, and with his eyes glimmering of hope, grabbed my hands waiting for my answer.

"I love you, so much." What came out of my mouth next would alter my foreseeable future. My whole life flashed before my eyes. "Yes! I will."

I was in love with Hayden and I couldn't deny that, but accepting his proposal shouldn't have taken so much convincing. Inside, I was afraid.

We took a flight to Honolulu the next morning and were married that afternoon.

The Promise

Something happens to a person on Oahu. I'm convinced that the purple haze effect is real. Like a narcotic scattering the horizon that causes you to take leaps of faith and make promises that you normally wouldn't; whether you mean them, or not.

At the time, Hayden meant every word.

We were both still a little hung over from champagne and being up all night, so we packed what we needed in a few bags and left the rest behind, rushing to make our flight to Honolulu.

I don't know how either of us thought that going to City Hall was a good idea.

"What can I do for...?" A fresh faced girl with pageant hair, but a contradictory nose piercing looked up, "Oh, my god! Hayden Jones...what are you doing in here?" The clerk couldn't have whispered any louder, before jerking her head in my direction. "You're getting married?" There were at least a half dozen other couples in the huge room, some in wedding dresses and suits, to my Ella Moss halter maxi dress and Hayden in jeans and a jacket. I don't think anyone else recognized him underneath that Lakers cap. "Hold on a second..." She left and quickly returned, waving for us to follow through the door behind her and down a hall where we ended up in a very official looking office.

In stepped a judge; a kindly looking man with thick, long eyelashes. He had on a suit but I was disappointed that he wasn't wearing a robe.

"Well, I wonder what you two need me for." He chuckled, before cutting his eyes to the clerk who gawked from the doorway. "Can you send Lyla in so that we can get the documents done?"

"Thank you, Sir. I want to marry this woman before she comes to her senses and changes her mind." Hayden joked and I nudged him.

"I won't, because I'm looking forward to the honeymoon."

The two men laughed, assuming I was joking.

On cue, Hayden pulled out the ring he had kept hidden all week.

My jaw dropped when I saw the Tiffany box. "What is this?" Looking up at him, I knew he had planned the entire thing. "You knew what you were doing all along." Hayden opened it, revealing a perfect solitaire diamond and platinum ring.

Hayden grinning, asked me again. "Will you marry me, Alexia?"

Laughing and crying, I jumped into his arms. "Yes, yes... I love you!"

The judge had to clear his throat because he probably got uncomfortable watching us kissing and just about making out in his office.

Quick and simple – we were out of there in fifteen minutes.

~

"Oh my god, yes!"

My hips gyrated steadily, taking all of him as orgasmic waves of ecstasy flowed through me, before falling limp across Hayden's chest. *Ahhh… no more faking it!* I gleefully thought.

"Baby!" Hayden, still inside of me, glanced down at his shoulder. "If you leave marks on me like that, the makeup team is going to have to cover it up." He then laughed, realizing how ridiculous that was.

"Then…stop doing that to me." I kissed his neck, and then squeezed my thighs, before lifting up. "Come on, we have to shower and get something to eat. We only have a few hours before we leave."

It seemed we had gotten by virtually unnoticed at The Royal Hawaiian hotel, where we hid out in our suite before flying back to Los Angeles on the red eye. In the middle of a romantic dinner in one of the restaurants,

Hayden caught me pushing the food around with my fork and just staring at my plate, my thoughts probably showing all over my face.

"You're still worried about all of this, aren't you?"

I felt stoned, like there was no way it was real. My entire life had shifted and then the reality of it all, just hit me. "No, but my parents are going to kill me." My eyes welled up in tears.

He reached over, holding my hand. "Here... I promise you, I'll fix it, okay?"

I couldn't believe I had done that to them. I'd last spoken to my parents the week before I left for Hawaii. My mother knew I was dating someone I referred to as Denny, but didn't know *who* he was. Hayden's mother lives in Santa Barbara, so I hadn't met her yet. We had a lot of fixing to do.

Back in our suite, Hayden professed his heart to me, on the lanai, in the presence of his favorite old school singers. He's not really one for our generation's ideal of great music. Hayden prefers to make love to The Isley Brothers over Usher. But, when he's in one of his blaze-one-up-and-shoot-the-shit-with-the-fellas moods, Lil' Wayne is the only acceptable choice, in his opinion. What does that tell you?

"Before we get back to LA, I want you to know that I will love you and take care of you forever. And, I'll never do anything to hurt you, Alexia. I promise you that."

I trusted Hayden and didn't have any reason to doubt him.

So back to LA we went. Hoping we could sneak in before the parents, managers, and the rest of the world found out.

Little did we know, though… all hell was about to break loose.

ACT II: Hollywood Ever After

"In Tinsletown dreams and nightmares are one in the same."

Glitter-Hooked

When I married Hayden, I didn't really know him in the truest sense; I admit that. But, I do know that I loved him; that is, everything I got to know about him in the short time we dated. The way I always felt relevant and special when I was with him. And, that I was comfortable with him, which is something I rarely felt with anyone. He knew my flaws and still held me on this unattainable pedestal. I would have never rejected his proposal. He'd surely take care of me in every way. We could fill in the blanks along the way.

Hayden and I got married because he had chosen me and wanted no one else to love me the way he planned to. And, he did love me like no one else could have. I was swept off my feet by the way he spoiled and showed me off around town.

Hollywood fell in love with me just as much. Alexia Jones was their latest focus: *Who's the sweet little temptress that married the box office hunk?* My name was inked on the lists of the most desired charities, fashion events and parties. I was kept pretty busy. So much so that I turned a blind eye to the chaos that my life was becoming.

Even with that said, I was open and responsive to all of it. I accepted the luncheon invitations, the free swag and clothes, and the gifts from people I had never even met. All because I was Hayden Jones' wife and they wanted or needed something from him. Unlike all the goodies I received from men before I met Hayden, half the time I would now send the good stuff to Barstow, so that Mom could enjoy it. Because I knew there were more to come.

I became one of the most photographed women in town. Everywhere we went, paparazzi were there. It made me self conscious, but over time, Hollywood glitter-hooked me. When she does that, there's no turning back. It becomes a way of life.

When we got off the plane at LAX, it was all downhill and I didn't see it coming.

So much for honeymooning

LAX Arrivals – 6am mayhem

$\mathcal{T}$he nervous airport security guard struggled to keep up with us as Hayden and I hurriedly exited the baggage claim door to the waiting sedan. He yelled at people to "…get out of the way!" I felt so bad. A uniformed police officer cleared the way as tourists craned their necks to see what the commotion was about. I could already see at least a dozen photographers outside.

The news was out.

Hayden, donning sunglasses, was unfazed by the relentless paparazzi, who were now shouting at us.

"Hayden! Hayden, over here!"

"What's her name?"

"Alexia, come on…this way! You may as well get used to this, sweetheart!" Trying to edge me on, the paparazzo's voice was forceful and chilling.

What did he say? And, how the hell did he know my name?

"I'm not your sweetheart, asshole!"

"Whoooaa… Nice, she's a hellcat. I like it!"

"Ignore him, baby." Shielding me, Hayden held my waist tightly as we made our way to the car. "That's enough!"

We were facing a sea of piranhas.

With my arm wrapped around Hayden's back, my fingers clutched onto his jeans pocket with every bit of strength I could muster.

"Who told them?"

I didn't dare to look into the cameras, but I didn't completely look away either. *I may as well let them see me now and get it over with* I thought. As terrified as I was, I also knew better than to hide my face. What would be the point? If I ducked and hid, they'd hound me until I really went off and then they'd eat me alive.

Hayden tried easing the moment, "Don't worry about it. They're hungry for the money shot." He pulled me closer in a protective hug as we approached the car.

I wasn't worried, just confused as to how the press had found out so quickly. We hadn't been married a day and the paparazzi were already clamoring at our heels. Surely there had to be something or someone more important than me to hound.

The driver rushed to open the door, "You're fine now, Ma'am..." I looked over my shoulder, climbing into the car, wondering how I'd survive as wife of one of the biggest movie stars in the world. I was a pro at handling pseudo hustlers and pretty boy rich kids, but this? It was like being in a bubble.

Hayden got into the car and seemed fine as he scrolled through his cell phone. Rusty had already sent a dozen messages.

"Did you hear me, Hayden?"

He glanced up, "No, I'm sorry...what's wrong?" He clinched his hand around mine.

"Why do they care, and who the hell leaked this?"

He just laughed, "Alex, anyone with a pulse. Think about it...we were married by a justice of the peace, in Hawaii of all places. You know that girl was on the phone as soon as we walked out."

"Dammit, so much for honeymooning!" I was annoyed but at the same time, a little excited by it all. Passing the big LAX monument as we exited the airport is when I was hit by the reality that I wasn't going back to my Rossmore apartment. I didn't know where I belonged at that point. "Where are we going?"

"Home." Hayden was so matter of fact when he announced it.

"Which one?" I pulled out a compact and blotted my flushed face.

Hayden tried being sympathetic. "Good question." He knew I wasn't ready yet to just dive into his existence.

"Well, can we go somewhere else for a couple of days? Neutral ground… until the shock settles and they lose interest."

"You're the boss." He called Kaz and told him to call the hotel and reserve a suite for the week. Then, instructed the driver. "Change of plans, my friend. We're going to the Marina."

I could feel myself relaxing. Maybe we'd actually have a chance to enjoy our first days in peace. Then…my phone rang. "Oh my god, it's Lilly."

"You're in for it now, girl." Hayden was amused by my panicked condition. "Go ahead, answer it. You may as well get this done." Rubbing his hand across my thigh tempted me to let the call go to voicemail.

"Here we go… Hey Lil, I was about to call you."

"Really?" Her voice oozed with sarcasm. "How was your vacation? Tell me all about it. What'd you do, Alex?"

"Well…" I stalled for a moment. "What did you hear?"

"That you ran off with that kick-boxing hunk to Hawaii and he married your ass!" Lilly played it cool, as if she was joking around; but, was covering up the fact that she was insulted that I had kept her in the dark. "Honestly Alex, why didn't you tell me that *he* was the guy you were seeing, and that it had gotten serious? We're supposed to be friends."

"I don't know…." All I could do was gaze at Hayden as a wave of guilt rushed over me. "Try to understand. I want all of us to get together real soon."

"Right. Okay well, congrats and …" Lilly paused like she was searching for words. "…tell Hayden I look forward to seeing him."

Lilly was hurt. I heard it in her voice. She would have to get over it. I hadn't told anyone. Not even Stacee, and she brought me to Hayden.

~

Exhausted from the flight and mayhem at the airport, the quick fifteen minute drive to the Marina lulled me to sleep, but I awakened when the door slammed. The driver was standing with his back against my door. I rolled the window down.

"Excuse me, what's going on?" I was aching to crawl into the first bed I could find.

"Oh yes, Miss." He addressed me as *Miss* like I was some girl Hayden had picked up. "I was asked not to wake you. He's inside and…"

I waved him to stop talking. "Alright..." Irritated by it all, I let the window back up. Just then, Hayden and the hotel manager approached the car and opened my door.

"Good morning Mrs. Jones, and welcome to The Ritz-Carlton." Though the man was quite proper and could have been intimidating, I noticed that behind his specs were kind eyes, with little crinkles at the corners.

"Hello, thank you." Muscling up a smile I rubbed my hands through my tousled hair as the polished, slightly feminine gentleman greeted me.

Holding a two-way radio in his hand, he continued. "I will be escorting you to your suite and please, whatever you need Mrs. Jones, we will work our best to accommodate."

Hayden shook the man's hands and then came to help me out of the car.

"How're you feeling?" He kissed me, gliding his thumb across my jaw.

Despite the fact that everything happened so fast, I knew Hayden truly loved and trusted me, because I turned out to be the girl who wanted *him*, not the Hollywood star.

"I'm good." I had never felt that kind of love for anyone - ever. "Will you always look at me the way you do right now?"

"Yes, because I'll *always* love you."

Following behind the hotel manager, I tried not to notice the few early rising guests who were taking pictures. I could hear their cameras clicking, but was too tired to care.

"This is what happens to gorgeous women. They get stalked." Hayden was so amused by all of it.

"Gorgeous? Yeah, right. I'm a mess and can't wait to get to a bath and more sleep."

"I know… me too."

As we walked through the lobby the staff greeted us with quiet smiles and plenty of discretion. The surroundings were so serene and beautiful, and our suite was as romantic as I expected. It had three terraces and fabulous marina views. For a while we had own little slice of Heaven away from the public.

I found Hayden lying on his back across the bed, exhausted.

"There you are." I lay on top of him.

Opening his eyes, he smiled. "Hi…" He wrapped his arms around my waist.

"So, how long are we staying here?"

"Until you're comfortable. Not to mention, I want you all to myself for a few days. We won't be bothered here."

I glanced up at the luxurious surroundings. "It's perfect."

"Besides, you'll need to build your courage to tell your parents what *you* did." With a mischievous chuckle under his breath, he smacked my butt, letting me roll onto the bed as he got up.

There was nothing funny about it. "Hayden we have to call them today - like, now! That includes your mom."

Hayden rolled his eyes and shook his head as he lifted the shirt over his head revealing his solid six-pack. "My mother won't be so shocked, trust me."

I wondered why Hayden would say that about his mom. Didn't she care about what happened in his life? The way it sounded, it would be business as usual.

All kinds of thoughts went through my head as I watched him pull the belt from his Citizens of Humanity jeans. He had close to a hundred pair lined up in his closet at home. Not surprising, because Hayden had the best looking ass in Hollywood and those jeans proved it. The fact that it now belonged to me was worth cherishing and could perk up any girl.

He undressed while I sat there with tears welling up in my eyes. Thinking *he's trying to have sex at a time like this*, the whole eloping news was going to be upsetting to a lot of people, and I knew it.

"Are you coming?" He walked off towards the shower. I sat on the edge of the bed moping while my hot husband was waiting for me. It didn't take more than ten seconds to snap out of it. For the time being.

~

"Who is that?"

I was startled awake in the middle of the night by a woman's voice. I was incoherent as is usually the case when I'm awakened from a deep sleep. Not wanting to let go of the bed, I had to find out why someone was singing. As I tried to slide out of bed quietly, I felt Hayden's leg entwined with mine. He laid there completely unfazed. Not even my loud whispers awakened him.

With my head spinning as I stood, the bottle of champagne from earlier was making me pay. It was then that I realized the irritating woman's voice was the stereo in the living room. A few tea lights still flickered on the patio. I took it all in and couldn't help but wonder how my life turned out like this. Does a girl really fall in love and marry a man she's only known for a couple of months and live happily ever after? I hoped so, because there was no turning back.

"Hey...why are you out here?" Hayden walked up behind me, draping a robe on my shoulders. "Here, it's cool out."

"Sorry. Did I wake you?" I enjoyed his hands caressing my neck; trying to hide my worried face.

"You're tense, what's wrong?" Hayden turned me to face him and that's when he saw I had been crying. "You're happy, aren't you?"

"Of course." I was shocked by his question. "Why would you ask that?"

Hayden knew what the issue was - my family. I was feeling a massive guilt of sneaking off and getting married without so much a word. What if the press had found out where my family lived, and blurted the news before I got to them? That was a possibility, and all of it concerned me. Even with that, I wasn't ready to call my parents.

"In a couple of days, we'll drive to Barstow. It'll be fine, you'll see."

"This is why I love you. You understand me and it doesn't scare you off." I giggled to lighten the moment. "You don't mind?"

"Why would I? I love you and it's important." He slid his hands under my robe. "Come back to bed."

I perched on my tip toes, draping my arms around Hayden's neck, kissing him deeply, encouraging his tongue to meet mine. "Why bother going back to bed?"

His hands caressed my skin, before finally sliding the robe off. My entire body quivered as he stroked my nipples. Leaning against the wall, I lifted a leg onto the sofa.

"Mmm…you're a bad girl. I love it…"

"You know by now, you don't have to be gentle. I can take it."

That was music to his ears, as his hand found home between my thighs.

"Let's see if you can." His kisses worked way down my chest, to my waist. Hayden knew that I was ready for what he was about to give.

"I belong to you, baby…" I purred, begging Hayden to move in. "…forever."

"Do you promise?"

"Yes! I promise… oh my god!"

We christened our newly merged lives, just before dawn, in ecstasy over Marina del Rey as subtle echoing of boat engines sounded out that early morning. Hayden gave it to me the way I liked it; aggressive and forceful and I introducing him to my hidden sexual prowess. We foolishly made love on that patio without a care as to who might be watching. It was those kinds of risky exhibitions that stimulated us the most.

I met my match in Hayden. He was my ideal husband and I was the girl he always wanted. Sexual games would prove to be no taboo in our house. We were more than attentive to our sex life, and became obsessed with pleasing each other.

This was just the beginning.

Pretty Caruso to the rescue

$\mathcal{N}$ot even two days of mind-blowing sex could dismiss the fact that our eloping would prove to be disappointing to my parents.

I could just hear my mother's voice: 'How could you? Why did you? I always dreamed of seeing you walk down the aisle...' The guilt trip Mom was notorious for was sure to come. My father – he would be different. He'd want to make sure I was being treated right. That Hayden, rich celebrity or not, truly loved me. I was his baby and he wouldn't stand for any less when it came to that.

"You ready, Alex?" Hayden, in Hollywood star mode, stood at the bathroom doorway of our suite in aviator sunglasses and his signature v-neck tee and jeans. Watching me as I sat at the vanity roughly tugging the brush through my hair, he could sense that I was anxious, and he walked over and hugged me. "I promise you, it'll be fine, okay?"

Looking up at Hayden, I nodded. "I know it will be. I just hope they don't act weird about us."

He laughed at the thought. "Honestly, they probably already know."

I swirled around in the chair. "You think?"

Hayden raised a brow. "No, I doubt it. Come on let's go. It's almost Noon and we have a long drive." No matter what he was saying, I knew there was a possibility that our news had already reached Barstow.

A familiar voice met us in the living room. "Look at you two!"

I couldn't believe it. There was Pretty Caruso, Hayden's right hand man assistant. I hadn't seen him since the party. I gave him a big kiss on the cheek. "Kaz! It's so good to see you. It's been a while."

"It sure has..." He had an inquisitive look on his face.

"Ummhmm...you know this is entirely your fault." I playfully smacked Kaz's arm, as he casually handed me his laptop. *What is this?*

"Hey, I just cleared the path for love."

"Oh, no!" I was stunned. "It's a stupid photo of me yelling in the camera at the airport." The headline on the gossip blog read *Can Hayden Jones tame his beautiful and fiery new wife?* "This is awful."

Kaz waved his hand. "Oh, never mind them." He turned attention to Hayden. "I've checked out already, and the Rover is out front."

Flipping his bag onto his shoulder Hayden nodded, "Alright, thank you, man."

"Not a problem - and Alexia, don't you worry about anything. I'm going to do my best to keep the vipers away from you."Addressing Hayden, he added, "That includes all crazy-ass managers."

Rusty Fisk had been trying to contact Hayden since we returned to LA. "You guys call me when you're on your way back from..." He glanced at me.

"Barstow."

"That's right!"

"Thank you, Kaz." I was impressed by his take charge manner. Kaz did whatever it took to secure Hayden's world, which now included me. "Okay, I think I'm ready." I wasn't, but didn't have a choice.

As the car approached the exit of the hotel, we spotted a few paparazzi waiting. Obviously they had been tipped off that we were checking out. *Who does this stuff?* Nothing is sacred in Hollywood and everybody's business is for sell.

"Hayden, I thought he meant they would be waiting for us when we got back from Barstow."

I flipped the sun visor down and patted some strawberry flavored gloss on my lips. I don't know what came over me, but I slyly glanced to my right and gave one of the paparazzo a sweet smile. Surprised by the gesture, he gave a thumb up and mouthed, *"Thank you..."*

I was becoming keen to what was necessary. Sometimes you have to connect with the other side; to the root of the stress. Keep your enemies close, they say. The press was bound to become our worst enemy. But, if I could charm some of them into loving me, instead of just waiting for me to fall... then they might just be on my side when I needed them most.

That day hopefully would never come - but just in case, I set up a little insurance.

Parents Slash Onlookers

"Nothing has changed here. Not one damn thing."

I pulled my sunglasses up and peered out at the mountainous desert town that I used to call home. It was still that, but only metaphorically. I instantly remembered why I left and it was a reminder to thank God again that I raged to get out of Barstow. The only part I missed was hanging with my old girlfriends. We all had the same dreams. As it turned out though, I was the only one to go after mine.

"It doesn't look that bad, Alex." Hayden grinned, rolling the window down at the stop light, checking out the scene. We were on the main thoroughfare complete with burger joints, a pancake house, lots of strip malls and fifty-nine dollar per night motels. He was fascinated. "I've never been up here. It's so real. I like it."

Just then Hayden noticed a little boy around ten years old in the car in front of us, leaning out of the back passenger window, staring at him, with a questionable look on his face.

"Alex, check out this kid."

Hayden was pretty sure the boy recognized him and hoped he didn't make a big deal. Leaning his head out of the driver window, Hayden gestured a *shhh* sign with his finger up to his lips. The boy giggled and waved, pulling back into the car.

"He's going to be talking about this forever." I laughed. "Oh my god, you have no idea what's about to happen." Combing my fingers through my hair and laying back against the rest, I pulled those sunglasses back over my eyes. I could feel my face getting hot. Just imagining my mother's reaction was over taking me. "We've been married three days without so much of a word and my parents are going to flip out; especially Mom."

Hayden couldn't relate to the burden I carried. He had decided to *maybe* call his mother in a few days and ask her drive to LA to meet me. She hadn't called him, so we thought she probably didn't know yet. Either that or she was so used to Hayden's pop-up surprises that hearing about it on TMZ was like, news at eleven. When Hayden Jones became a twenty million per picture movie star, even his mother became a parent slash onlooker.

"You're over reacting." Reaching over to grab my hand Hayden assured me there was no reason to be worried. He'd make sure to block any imposed guilt tossed my way. "Your parents love you, baby, and they'll see how much I do, as well."

Hayden's smile calmed me and I knew it would all work out. Much to do about nothing, I thought. "I love you too and I know you're right." We were approaching the neighborhood. I directed him ahead. "The house is coming up. Turn right at the light and the road continues around the curve entering the subdivision."

Reaching to the back seat, I blindly sifted through my bag and pulled out my makeup compact. I felt the need to look my best and give a sense of confidence so that Mom and Dad couldn't feed off my inward guilt.

~

Mom flung the door open, a split second after I pressed the bell.

"I was wondering when you two would show up to explain yourselves."

"What?" My voice was shallow. It's like I couldn't say anything; just receive my mother's glare.

Hayden let go of my hand and hugged his mother-in-law. "Mrs. Diamond, it's a pleasure. Finally..."

My mother squeezed him back, then grabbing both of us by the hands, her tone changed, "Why so formal? I'm Gabby, now get yourselves in here." She looked past us as if checking to see if any neighbors were watching.

I sighed a little. "Mom, how did you find out?"

"You're kidding me, right?" Gesturing she proclaimed, "Girl, look at your man. He's not exactly the paper boy you know. News travels fast around these parts."

Hayden amused by Mom's frankness, felt right at home. "You're a lovely lady and now I know where Alex gets her beauty."

"Well I didn't think you'd find out so fast. It's only been a few days." I hoped Mom wouldn't start to cry or anything. "I'm sorry. I wanted to call..." Then I looked up and saw my father walk into the room. "Daddy, hi!" I rushed over to him and was met by comforting arms.

Good thing Hayden was confident, because my father could easily make him feel like he'd stolen his daughter away. I could tell he was nervous in the presence of my father.

"Well, well...Hayden Jones in the flesh - In my house. Married to my daughter! How 'bout that?"

Paul Diamond is burly, yet gentle. Still he was the type who knew how to intimidate with just the right words, no matter how dignified. And, it worked.

Hayden took a couple of steps forward, with an outreached hand. "Sir, it's good to meet you...really."

Dad shook his hand, with a cool nod. It didn't look good.

"Why are we all still gathered at the front door?" He gestured for us to sit down. "Make yourself at home Hayden...because we all have to relax eventually."

"Paul, leave him be!" Closing the door, I'm sure Mom knew Dad was about to drill the man who had the nerve to marry his daughter *without* his consent.

"Gabby, you know we both want to hear the story of how this all happened. And, so quickly."

Next thing I know, I flung my purse across the room, where it landed on a chair in the corner. I was fed up with the tip-toeing. "Okay -what?" My arms stretched to the sky. "I got married, so what!" My mouth hanging open like I was waiting for a big response.

Hayden gave a remorseful glance to me, "Babe..." Then visually summoned back up from my mother.

"Alright, alright. Let's all sit and calm down." My mother was anxious to hear how her daughter ended up married to a man she'd only know on the big screen. Then she disappeared to the kitchen to make tea. I don't know if she was star-struck or what, but I expected a lot worse from her.

My stare followed Mom until she turned the corner. That's when I broke down. "Daddy, I'm sorry." Elbows on the dining table, I clutched my hands together.

"Sorry, for what?" Dad looked at Hayden, "Does your family know?"

"I don't know." Hayden said quite frigidly. "Maybe."

"Maybe?" Though it seemed odd to my dad, that fact made him feel better, I think. "We'll all get over it. You ran off, so…it's done. Worst things are happening in life."

I was surprised by my dad's reaction. I'm sure Hayden was waiting for either the other shoe to drop or a fist across his face.

"I took Alexia back to Hawaii, where I spent time, growing up. Then we just decided we wanted to be together and I asked her. Lucky for me, she said yes."

Dad listened and watched Hayden as he spoke. "You love my daughter?"

Feeling uncomfortable for Hayden, I knew my father was phishing for truth in his eyes and words. Dad is like a lie detector. Especially when it comes to me.

"More than my own life. She *is* my life now." Just then Hayden's cell beeped and he clicked it off. "But I won't lie; it's going to be tough on us both. My job and all…"

"Your *job*." Chuckling Dad continued, "You're a damn movie star, Son." Slapping the table, Dad made his statement understood. "Don't play it down – you've earned it!"

Hayden glanced over at me and winked, inducing a glimmer of a smile from my nervous soul.

Mom reappeared holding a tray of drinks. "Tell me, what did I miss?"

"Nothing, Mom. Just that… we love each other and didn't want to wait."

"Be sure to call your parent's right away, Hayden. They're probably as shocked as we are."

"Well, my father passed away, but Mom… yeah, I'll be getting an ear full any minute now."

Trying not to look uncomfortable because of her unknowing blunder, Mom was quick to apologize. "Sweetheart, I'm sorry, I…"

"No don't be, it was a long time ago."

"But, I know you're in love. I can sense it." Glancing at Dad to show unity, "We're happy for you two children."

"Really, Mom?" I jumped up and hugged her. Whispering in her ear, "I thought about you guys the whole time."

I really hadn't, but I wanted my mother to feel a part of the whole decision. She rubbed my back like she did when I was little.

Hayden and I stayed with my parents that night, sleeping in my old room. As soon as possible in the morning we drove back to Los Angeles. I didn't want to stay another day in Barstow. The house would have eventually become packed with relatives and friends who *happened* to be in the neighborhood.

It was time to face the music of married life and I knew that. Triple that by the fact that I would from that moment on, live in a fishbowl. Though I wanted to, there was no putting it off.

The Kinship of Miss Sylvie

$\mathcal{I}$t felt strange walking into the Kimridge Road house. I was no longer Hayden's guest, or his girlfriend and it wasn't an overnighter. It was now *our* home which is probably why I prolonged going to either place after Hawaii, but chose to stay in a hotel. But, now it was time for realness of being Mrs. Hayden Jones, to set in. The thought of everything that came along with that title was extremely nerve-wracking.

Sylvie met us at the door. "I wasn't expecting you until tomorrow." Clasping her hands she turned to me with a huge smile. "Welcome home, Mrs."

I hugged her. "Thank you, but come on now Sylvie… I told you, please call me Alex." I instantly felt a kinship with Sylvie. Those Bahaman roots, I suppose.

Hayden followed, "Madame Sylvie…" Hugging her he teased, "You know I asked you to manage this place because I secretly wanted to marry *you*."

Giggling, Sylvie gave him a maternal smack on his shoulder, "Stoppit now, boy…"

Leaving our bags at the door, Hayden grabbed my hand, leading me up the stairs. It had been a grueling couple of days and at this time I really just wanted to disappear with my husband and leave the world outside because I had a feeling the time was limited. My life was no longer private and my husband enjoyed his movie star lifestyle to the hilt, which meant I could expect lots of invasion of privacy. Only when we were home, would I have him all to myself.

Home – which one was that, again?

Simple tasks such as unpacking my bags were daunting. I didn't know where to put them. His closet, guest closet…where?

I moved very few of my things to Kimridge Road and had planned to get over to my apartment and slowly pack up the rest to put in storage. There was no idea whatsoever what I was going to do with the Rossmore apartment. Hayden told me not to worry about it; that there was no hurry to get rid of the apartment. Even suggesting I might like having it available for getaway time if I needed it. I thought *why would I need or even want getaway time?* We had just said I Do, so that definitely was not a good idea.

~

Word was Hayden was moody. Who told me that? Why, Miss Sylvie, of course.

"That boy's mind changes like the wind." She fanned her slim arms in the air, "One way, then turns another. You'll get used to it." She assured me.

Sylvie and I had quite a few little chats about life in Hayden's crazy world. "You're a young girl, but all the same, you're the woman of the house now, so set your heel down. You hear me?"

She told me never to let anyone come into my home, especially not 'those Hollywood people', and try to run over me. Then, after scaring me with all of that, she says, "But, Hayden loves you. I've never seen him so happy. You're good for him. Just remember what I say."

I felt safe in that Hayden loved me, but like she said, I was a young girl and now had a husband to care for. Let's face it, Sylvie's burden was lifted and now it was all on me to listen to and take on Hayden's baggage. I had to up my game to be ready for that.

Sylvie was like a guru slash Bahaman mother. Hayden trusted and listened to her. I treasured that she liked me because I had a feeling I would need her comforting at some point.

The friendship paradox

When I got back to LA, I knew a sit-down with Lilly was unavoidable. She didn't understand and was pissed at me. Not because I got married, but because I held the most monumental event of my life, secret from her. Falling in love and then getting married. Lilly and I had been through some seriously questionable times together and now I had shut her out. That's how she felt.

Then, I found the email.

Hayden tried to persuade me to call Lilly when we returned home, but, I was afraid to. *I don't know what to say. I'll call tomorrow*, I replayed the excuses in my head.

Hayden told me I should have called Lilly from Hawaii but I couldn't do that. How do you tell your best friend that you've gotten married? *I'm fine... trip is good... oh, I just got married... I bought you a souvenir...* I was more scared about seeing her than I had been about my folks.

Finally, after two days of being home, I called her. That's where it got weird. Lilly was always just a phone call away. I rarely got a voicemail. This time though, there was no answer, no call back - nothing. That told me, she was upset.

Later in the week I got a text.

I got your message. It's crazy right now. Get with

you soon.

- Lilly.

Just...Lilly? It felt cold. She had always ended her messages with *Love, Lil.* I called Jerzy.

"Why won't she call me, Jerzy? I've been trying to reach her every day."

"Lilly's not ready to talk yet. She said last night, 'Alex isn't the friend I thought she was.'" Those words cut deep. "Hey, she didn't mean that. Her feelings are hurt, that's all. Give her time, she'll come around."

Jerzy tried to make me feel better about it. Still, hearing those words hurt my heart. One of the few friendships I had was finished because I got married? I was so down about it that Hayden urged me to go to her.

"Don't call her, just go over there. She'll be alright. It's not like you killed somebody."

Hayden just didn't get it.

My life had changed overnight and with Hayden's demanding schedule, I would surely become lonely, really quick. I needed Lilly back.

So, I took his advice and went to her. What would she do, slam the door in my face?

~

Driving along the winding curves of Thrasher Avenue, my mind played over the paradox of our relationship. Lilly moved in with Jerzy quicker than she could blink her mink eye lashes. I found out from Erik, of all people. Then she justified it by saying, 'You know these things go, Alex.' Now – she was upset with me for moving in with *my* man. Only, I was married when I did it. I got upset just thinking about the nerve.

I was thankful that the gate was already open. I got out of the car, stomping my Prada pumps all the way to the door; digging my thumb nail into my palm while I waited for someone to come to the door. Surprisingly, Lilly showed up almost immediately, like she knew I was coming. Her hair was piled on top of her head in a messy ponytail and she was wearing yoga pants and a tank. I'd obviously interrupted her.

When the door opened we just stared at each other for what seemed like minutes, though it was only seconds.

"Hey." Lilly had a blank look on her face, pulling her ponytail loose. "I wish I knew you were coming. You should have called."

"Yeah, well I tried that." Tucking my clutch underneath my arm, I waited. "Why haven't you returned my calls?"

She turned and walked away. "Come in Alex, we're not standing at the door."

I looked around the museum-like living room and then out the glass doors that led to the backyard. I wondered if Jerzy was home. I hoped not.

"So, how you been? Is everything okay?"

Lilly scrunched her face and shrugged, "Of course, why wouldn't it be?" She was frigid towards me. I didn't deserve that.

"Lilly, stop!" I was tired of dancing around the issue.

With her hands on her bony hip she blasted me. "What? What am I supposed to say? (in a mocking tone) - Oh congratulations, I'm so happy... So happy you got married to someone you've known a couple months and even when I spoke to you before that, you never mentioned it was *him* you were going out with. Alex - I found out from TMZ. That's bullshit!"

My eyes welled up. Sitting on the sofa, I felt like a five year old being scolded. "I'm sorry it went down like that and you're hurt. But, I'm not apologizing for marrying Hayden. And now, Jerzy tells me you're not sure about our friendship. What is that?"

She sat next to me on the sofa trying to show some understanding. "I know, it's just...I felt left out." Not giving in, Lilly held back the emotion that I saw building in her eyes. She was disappointed and I felt bad about that.

"Left out of what?" My eyes pleaded with her. "I need to know we're good."

The pause was long and isolating. I didn't know what her response would be. I waited, reading her facial expression that usually told all. This time I couldn't tell.

She hugged me. "Look, I'm always here for you and to prove it, I want us all to have dinner tomorrow night. I mean, if Hayden's okay with it."

"Of course, he's okay with it. He knows how much this means to me, and just wants me to be happy."

"Great. I'll make reservations at BOA. It'll be a nice time."

"BOA?" I laughed. "Maybe we should just set up a table at the intersection of Hollywood and Vine and have dinner there."

"Well, you may as well get this type of press out of the way. Besides, it'll be fun."

Leaving Lilly's that afternoon I was relieved that we got over that initial hurdle. It would definitely be uncomfortable in the beginning, but no matter, I was glad to know she was still on my team for the time being.

Is she for good?

*T*he Range Rover came to a slow roll approaching

BOA on Sunset Boulevard and I could already see the paparazzi perched out front. Let's face it, Lilly chose that place because it was like my coming out, of sorts. Baptism by fire. It's one of the most paparazzi swarmed restaurants in Hollywood and celebrities go there for one reason – to be seen.

"You may as well embrace it, Alex. Let 'em fall in love with you. After that, you won't really notice them."

Hayden fed me that line as we walked out of the house. He knew I was worried about being spoon fed to the public. He was right, though. The sooner I got splashed all over the blogs, the quicker people would either love or hate me. Then hopefully, get bored and leave me alone. Hayden Jones had married an unknown, and that's where the pressure came in. My every move would be under a microscope.

Thank God Lilly was there. She always had my back and told me earlier, "You're married to a movie star. Let them see you and get a few photos. But, no talking to the animals – ever."

Animals? Where did that come from? I assumed that was some Jerzy Friedman Hollywood lingo she picked up.

I was prepared to give them what they wanted. I chose a snug and plunging Roberto Cavalli dress plus my wedding ring in clear view. It was just enough to fill up a few gossip columns: *Makeup artist marries Hollywood star. Was there a pre-nup? Did she talk him into the quickie marriage? Is Alexia pregnant? Check out the rock!*

"Thank you, man." Hayden handed the keys to the valet as the blinding flashes popped off around us. "Hi, guys!"

He took it in stride and engaged the paparazzi as he walked around to the passenger side, where Jerzy had already opened Lilly's door. The two of them were at the sidewalk as Hayden helped me out.

While I knew the paparazzi would be at the restaurant, it was suspicious as to why they didn't seem surprised that it was Hayden pulling up. Everything was queued.

I tightly held onto Hayden's hand and he gave mine a comforting squeeze while my name was being shouted out by strange men. *Why do they even care?* I thought. *Hayden is the star, not me.* He was familiar with a couple of them and they kept a safe distance, not to cross the line. All, except one, that is.

"Hayden Jones! The Hollywood player finally settles down. Again!" The slimy jerk was taunting us, and Hayden tried ignoring him; wrapping his arm around me as we made our way towards the entrance of the restaurant. "This one's stunning, Hayden. Is she for good?"

Hayden stopped his stride. "Watch your mouth!" I had never seen him so aggravated.

Lowering his camera, the guy laughed, "Or what?"

"You heard me."

"That guy's a prick, Hayden. Not worth it, man." Jerzy saw the fire in Hayden's eyes.

A couple of restaurant staff opened the doors for us and one of them yelled out the door. "You guys, stay at the curb. Don't come near this door!"

~

"Hayden....Alex...I just want to say I'm glad we're all here tonight." Lilly looked at Jerzy as if she was soliciting more coaching.

"Congratulations to you both. It's a time to celebrate!" The server brought out a vintage bottle of Dom to the table.

"Yes, it is!" Lilly's face lit up and her cheerleader smile froze on Hayden. It was almost uncomfortable, but she was doing a good job of covering her feelings. I knew she was trying.

"Thank you, we appreciate you guys." Hayden draped one arm behind me in our booth. "Jerzy, it's been a long time, man. Where've you been?"

The two became acquainted years before when Hayden signed a multi picture deal with Paramax Studios. They would always do the Hollywood dance on the red carpet and at parties; but weren't really friends.

"I'm making it happen and keeping out of trouble with my girl here." Flashing his perfectly veneered smile, Jerzy responded with a rightful answer. But, in other words - he was up to nothing. After two years he should have sealed some type of real commitment to Lilly, even if *she* was fine with being his kept live-in.

Dinner was a courteous back and forth of friendly conversation mixed with occasional nice-nasty jabs, courtesy of Lilly. She blamed Hayden for what she felt was being left out when we got married. The more drinks she slurped back, the more sarcastic she became.

"I need to go to the ladies room, and I want you to come with me, Lil." Smiling, I winked at her and she scooted out of the booth, tugging the hem of her one shoulder metallic David Meister dress. I give her; she looked hot in that dress. Lilly knew how to dazzle, but her behavior was upsetting me and it was time to nip it in the bud.

No sooner than the door closed and making sure we were alone, I let her have it.

"What is wrong with you? I thought this was all good."

"Nothing! We're having a great time." She stood in the mirror, stroking her hair and trying not to look drunk.

"Let's see. What did you say? 'She's all yours now... the glamorous lock-down...' What the hell was that, Lilly?"

"Oh god, Alex, it's nothing, I was kidding around." She put her hand on my shoulder. "We're enjoying ourselves and you pull me in here for this?"

"And, to think Hayden talked me into seeing you, because he saw how upset I was over hurting my friend." I pushed her hand away. "Don't do this again, or I'm done!"

"Alex, come on..."

"I'm serious. You don't have to like him, but don't try to punish us because you weren't there to fluff my veil." I walked out of the bathroom and left her standing there.

Back at the table, I whispered to Hayden, "Can we

leave? I'm tired."

He looked up as Lilly was walking back to the table, with her pasted on smile. "Of course, let's go."

As we all gathered ourselves to leave, Jerzy declared, "We're going to do this again, soon."

Dinner was so uncomfortable, that I didn't even notice the paparazzi on the way out.

The night was a complete bust.

Feel better now?

Staring at the ceiling, I was overcome by a negative rush that made no sense. I felt like I was becoming the referee in a Hayden verses Lilly competition.

I know Hayden did the whole dinner with Lilly and Jerzy thing to make me happy. A night out with my friends was just another appointment. He didn't care about relationships the way I did, but he loved me. That meant doing what it took to make sure I was content and happy in my new life.

Hayden thought he had really done a good deed with this dinner. I'm always proud to be on his arm. What woman wouldn't be? He always made me feel like the queen and enjoyed showing me off. But, when it came to Lilly, there was something about our friendship that Hayden needed to keep in check. It was like he was jealous that Lilly knew me first, and surely knew secrets that I would never share with him; secrets that are covered under Girlfriend Code. Your husband does not need to know about everyone and every experience of your past. I'm sure that fact bothered him, and, is probably why he said what he did on the way home that night.

"Feel better now, Alexia?"

I looked out the car window, watching Jerzy close the door to their house. "Feel better about what?"

It was becoming very clear to me that Hayden Jones didn't like sharing his possessions, which now included me.

"That you got to spend some time with your friend." He said it like he had just performed some charitable act.

Gliding my thousand-dollar, designer toe-pinchers off my throbbing feet, I turned towards him with my head on the rest, "I enjoyed myself tonight, yes. It started out crazy with the paparazzi but... I have to get used to that, I suppose."

"They're mostly harmless. But yeah, you're going to be all over the magazines." His dimpled smile beamed like he was proud of the possibility.

"God, I hope not. Well, maybe just a little." I giggled but deep down, hoped he was wrong. "So, you didn't mind? Tonight, I mean."

"No." He reached over and rubbed my face while his eyes focused on the tricky curves of Sunset Plaza Drive. "As long as my wife is happy, I'll take time out for anything."

Nothing about that statement was soothing. It was so superior. I don't think I said a word to Hayden for the rest of the drive home.

Hayden was far removed from my friends and anything that related to my life before meeting him. The only person he truly tolerated was Stacee and that's because they were acquaintances before I came in to the picture.

As for his friends, there really weren't any. Not friends that you could count on to be there whether his career was on top or not. Hayden only felt comfortable socializing with other celebrities. He didn't trust anyone in the truest sense, but it's like fellow celebs were the familiar of two evils. Those he referred to as 'real-life people', didn't interest him on a personal level.

To this day, I don't understand how he let his guard down enough to want to marry me.

Life's a Hermosa Beach

When the phone next to the bed rang at seven
in the morning it terrified me. Someone's dead or in jail.
I just got married — do not freaking ruin this for me.
Selfishly, I didn't know which would upset me more.
Depends on whether it was family, I suppose. All of that
played out in my head in the five seconds after that first
ring.

Groggy from the something-or-another pill I took to
help me sleep, I rolled over staring at Hayden lying still
as a log. How was he still asleep? Something told me not
to dare wake him though, regardless of how afraid I was
to answer the call.

I grabbed the receiver, perching on my elbows.
"Yeah, hello?" I whispered as loudly as possible.

"Alexia! Hello, honey?" The woman's voice on the
other end was loud and drenched in southern charm.

"Yes...who is this, please?"

"It's your mother-in-law, Mareena, sweetie!"
Hayden's mother called me every pet name in the book
as she announced that she would be coming in from
Santa Barbara. She relocated to California after Hayden's
father died, because being in Atlanta was too painful,
with memories of her husband at every turn. So, she

decided to take on a new phase in life. "I know it's early but I just wanted y'all to know that I'll be there this afternoon." *This couldn't wait until later?* "I decided I had to get out there, because Lord knows it'll take my son a year to bring you here."

"Oh, it's so great to hear from you. I'm so sorry, I... My god..." I quickly sat up, leaning against the headboard. Smacking Hayden's arm, I was panicked. "I wish I had known, so I'd have everything ready."

"No need, baby, it's fine. I'm staying at the Hermosa Beach house, so don't you worry about a thing. Now, go back to sleep, Alexia and tell my son, Mommy will see him tomorrow. Or, I guess later today, right?" She giggled and sent kisses through the phone.

Mommy?

"Okay, I can't wait to see you. Alright...bye." As the call ended, I felt like I'd been sideswiped by a minivan. "Hayden! Your mother is on her way."

"Well, that's my mother for you." Laughing under his breath, he claimed he told me she was coming to LA. "Didn't I tell you I talked to her last week?" He knew he hadn't. "Mareena has to see you for herself."

Hayden rolled over and fell back to sleep just that quickly. By this time, hearing him refer to his mother by her first name didn't seem odd.

After a failed attempt, I couldn't sleep anymore. I got up, went to the kitchen and poured myself an orange juice.

Relaxing on the patio enjoying the dewy morning, everything was so still. I could see the peaks of the neighboring homes, beyond the hedges. Not a soul stirred over Beverly Hills and everything was quiet. I loved it - just me and a few birds chirping to welcome another day.

Then it occurred to me: *She has a beach house?* But then, why wouldn't she? Hayden always took great care of his mother. Mumbling to myself, I wondered what Mareena Jones would be like, and if she would like me. Mothers just come with the territory, I tried convincing myself. *I don't care if she doesn't approve of me.* Of course I cared. It was extremely important to me that our families loved both of us. Life would be so much easier. Or so I thought.

~

"So your mother – she seems very um...excitable."

Sylvie had fixed brunch for us, but my stomach was in knots. I couldn't eat a thing; just nursed a frothy fruit drink.

"To say the least." Half listening to me while skimming through a script he'd just received, Hayden forked over his banana French toast his darling Sylvie made just for him, since he doesn't eat eggs. "She's a free spirit, my mother - Like you." He glanced up from the script, giving me a cute grin.

"We'll get along great, then!" Reaching over and playfully smacking the script in his hands, I went over to his side of the table, draping my arms around his neck. "I'm meeting Lilly at Sunset Plaza. Call me if you need me, okay?" He leaned back for a lingering kiss which earned me a playful smack on my rear end as I walked off.

"What if I *need* you now?" He beckoned from the patio, peering into the kitchen, over his sunglasses.

I giggled, blowing him a kiss. "Bye!"

Zooming along Kimridge Road, with Jamiroquai blasting from the speakers, I was excited to meet Lilly for a little shopping and lunch. In other words, private girl talk. There was much need for reinforcements before meeting Hayden's mother. I swear, if Lilly and I had met for lunch on the moon that would have been fine by me. I was riddled with nerves over meeting his mother. Only Lilly could help me see the light. She'd tell it like it was.

And, that she did.

Swinging her crossed leg back and forth as a few paparazzi at the curb zoomed into our conversation, Lilly set the matter straight.

"Those guys love their girl Alex-iaaaa..." She tried covering her mouth with her glass.

"Don't look out there, Lilly. They'll leave in a minute."

"No, they won't!" She put the glass down and scooted her chair closer to the table and looked me square in the eye. "You don't know the power position you're in right now, do you?"

Just then I recognized one the guys; it was the photographer who snapped my mug at The Ritz-Carlton. I looked away and quietly grinned, removing my fitted cardigan and revealing the tank top. I thought I may as well be accommodating. "Lil, it doesn't feel that way."

"You're the girl who got Hayden Jones to stop screwing around." Lilly was still louder than she needed to be, and was two seconds from pissing me off.

"Why do you have to say that about him?"

Lilly laughed, "Okay, well he was notorious for his *extracurricular* activities. But, now he's off the market and in love with you, Alex. That's got everyone in this town itching to know who you are and what you've got that put a guy like Hayden on lock. And THAT my dear… his dear ol' Mom can't even do! You hold the power - point blank. She has no choice but to like you."

Lilly had put some thought into that sermon. I sure hoped she was right.

~

When I returned home, Hayden was pulling out just as I was about to turn into the gate. I waved him down.

"Where are you going?"

"Hermosa Beach. My mother is having a fit." He looked frustrated. "Are you coming?"

Though I was nervous to see his mother, I was more ready to get past it. "Yes, just let me park, okay?"

He backed back into the driveway and waited. I could see him watching me in his side mirror as I approached.

I climbed in and he drove off just that quickly. "What's going on, is she alright?" I caressed his shoulder.

Hayden glanced at his image in the rear view mirror as we drove off. Then leaned over and gave me a kiss. "I love you."

"I love you, too, babe."

"There's nothing wrong. My mother is spoiled rotten. She said, 'I've been here three hours and you haven't come to the house to see your mother.'" Hearing him mock her, I sensed he wasn't kidding.

I laughed, "Aw, stop. She just wants to see her baby boy."

"No, the person she really wants to see is you. I was just about to call you to meet me out there."

"Why didn't she just come here for dinner? Sylvie and I would have set it all up."

"No... we have to go to *her*. You'll understand. But, you'll love my mother, just as much as much as she will you. Like I said, you're a lot alike."

That didn't sound like me at all, but I hoped we would hit it off. Any woman who threw a tantrum because her son hadn't been waiting at the city limits when she arrived, would surely not be an easy introduction. I had around thirty minutes to brace myself.

"Why'd she get a place way out in Hermosa Beach?"

"I thought she'd enjoy living closer to the ocean. My mother would be at our house all day, every day if she were any closer."

The more he said about her, the more possessive she seemed. What kind of inappropriate, obsessive Motherdom was I about to encounter? I dreaded the thought.

Parental Guidance

"Mom, we're here. Yes, I'm pulling up right now." Hayden's dry conversation with his mother sent so many questions through my mind. "Of course, she's with me." I watched his eye roll as she kept talking.

"What's she saying?" I whispered loudly, watching him as if he would actually tell me with her being within earshot.

"Okay, see you in a minute."

We pulled up to the bi-level Mediterranean townhouse on Palm Drive and I thought *No wonder she's so demanding; because she can be.* The house was directly across from the ocean. The area seemed a lot easier going than Beverly Hills or even Malibu; less celebrity hungry and because of that, I fell in love with it. It's funny that I married one of the biggest movie stars in the world and became less impressed by anything Hollywood had to offer. He was a magnate for the tabloids, and while he took it in stride, I feared it.

Walking up those steps, I craved a glass of wine to take the edge off. I wished I could be more excited.

Mareena flung the door open. "Hayden!" Flinging her arms out, hugging him, Mareena looked over his shoulder, and straight into my eyes.

I was immobilized by her stare and wanted to run the other way. It was a long moment, as she squeezed him. The whole time I couldn't help but think how much his mother looked like Diane Keaton. Blunt bobbed haircut and all. Only her hair was dark brown, naturally or otherwise. Her figure was impressive for a woman in her late fifties. She was wearing a cleavage-revealing top and A-line skirt, with a scarf draped around her neck. *Pretty stylish*, I thought. Not what I imagined when I spoke to her earlier that morning.

"And, look at my daughter-in-law. Come here, darlin'." She pulled back from her precious offspring and reached for me.

A sigh pushed its way past my smile. "Mrs. Jones, hello." I was relieved the woman didn't choose to ignore me.

"You are as pretty as can be." Mareena's every sentence felt like the other shoe would drop at any moment. It was very overwhelming.

Hayden looked pleased that his mother was so welcoming to me. Still, he walked off while we hugged, looking around the space. "How was your drive, Mom?"

Mareena clutched my hand, "It was lovely, as usual. So - I thought we could all go to dinner; someplace quiet, and nearby if you don't mind."

Hayden sat down on one of the sofas, with his leg crossed over his knee, and arms stretched over the back. "That's fine, whatever you want, Mom."

The chilly interaction between Hayden and his mother was starting to make me feel as if I needed to step aside so they could hash out their differences. He was almost rude to her.

We ended up at the Bottle Inn, a cozy place where celebrities can pretty much blend in with the regular folks. We walked in without incident. But of course, when Mareena requested to be seated in the wine cellar, which is usually booked, we were escorted there immediately. Regular folks…right.

"You are going to love it here, Alexia. It's so charming. "

Immediately I was endeared to Mareena. She didn't seem like the spoiled and demanding woman Hayden made her out to be. Yet, it had only been an hour, so there was still time.

"Alexia, I can't tell you how much seeing this smile in my son's eyes, means to me. He's all work, but this… you've brought something to his life."

Mareena glanced at Hayden, while she stirred the olive around in her martini.

"Thank you, Mareena. We're both lucky to have found each other."

She shook her head. "Luck has nothing to do with it. I don't believe in that. This is a blessing, that's what this is. You both look happy."

Hayden reached over and caressed my back. "You're right, Mom. I don't know what I did to deserve her."

Mareena watched me the whole time Hayden and I talked about how we met, up to our eloping in Hawaii. It's like she was waiting for a glimmer of deceit in my eyes. Her approving smile put me at ease. She liked me and that was more than I could have hoped for.

Two teenagers, apparently brother and sister, who were sitting with their family against a far wall had been watching us, and then when they caught me staring back, walked over and asked Hayden for his autograph. He asked them if they had a camera phone. The boy almost fell as he ran back to their table; their father tossing his cell phone to him. Hayden scooted his chair back and the kids stood on either side of him. All three were grinning and holding up peace signs while I took the picture.

"Now, send that to all your friends."

Even though I know that he was not in the mood for interruptions, Hayden would never hurt a kid's feelings and disappoint them. He could be very gracious like that.

"Oh my god… Thank you Hayden Jones!"

They were so cute, the way they called him by his full name. They could barely contain themselves as the dad typed into his phone.

I swirled bread into olive oil while my mind tried to conjure up anything to talk about. The conversation needed to stay easy. "How long will you be in LA for, Mareena?" Small talk has never been my specialty, but I put my best foot forward.

"Only for a couple of days, then I'm off to Catalina with my girl friends. Have you been? If not, you must."

"You thought I had a sit down and knit type of mother, didn't you, Alex?" Hayden aimlessly flipped through the wine menu.

Mareena waved him off, "Stop that. I try to enjoy life. Besides, it keeps me out of your hair, Hayden."

He quickly glanced up, "Mom."

My head went back and forth like I was watching a tennis match.

"It's true." She then looked at me. "He doesn't like my babying, but somebody has to keep him grounded.

Now… he has you." Finishing off her martini, Mareena winked at me. Was she being sarcastic or genuinely relieved that he had someone to love and take care of him? "I like you Alexia. You came from good people, I can see that. Try to stay that way, because I'll tell you… Hollywood can change a girl, for the worse. It happened with his first wife." She spoke frankly, as if Hayden wasn't even sitting there.

"Mom, please!"

Mareena threw her hands up. "Hayden, I'm just telling her. I don't want this poor girl to get caught off guard. You know how these people can be." She continued. "You always look out for yourself Alexia, you hear me?" As Mareena kept on, I drifted off as those very words from my friend Erik subconsciously echoed through my head. *Make sure you always take care of yourself…* For only a second, I wondered where he was, and how he was. "And, I'm sure your mother would agree. Speaking of, I can't wait to meet her."

Snapping out of my daze, I rubbed Hayden's firm bicep. "Thank you Mareena, and yes, I would love that. My mother will be here from Barstow soon." Inside, I hoped it wouldn't be a disaster.

"Fabulous!" Mareena's speech was starting to slur, and the food hadn't even arrived.

When we got back to the beach house, I walked in on Hayden and Mareena in a heated discussion. Hoping it wasn't about me, I couldn't have done a quicker pivot out of the room because I didn't want to be involved. All I heard was Mareena's voice yelling, "… and don't you forget it!"

I poured a glass of wine, walked out the front door, and sat on the top step gazing at the sun setting on the ocean as cars drove by and couples walked along the beach. The wine, my third glass of the night, was now hitting me and I was getting upset with every elevated voice I heard coming from inside the house. The door was cracked just enough, then Hayden pulled it open.

"Say goodnight, if you have to. " He put his sunglasses on and it was nearly dark. "I'm not dealing with this shit. I'm out!"

I looked up and watched him stomp down the steps and to the car. "What's going on?" Perching myself up, I went back inside. "Mareena?"

She was standing at the kitchen island with her head resting in her hand. Then, hearing my voice, she looked up with a forced grin, fluffing her bangs to the side. "Alexia, sweetheart."

Keeping neutral, I hugged her, knowing she needed it. "I enjoyed this." I didn't dare ask her what happened.

My thinking was, try to let the night end of a peaceful note with a mother-daughter-in-law hug. There would be plenty of time to discuss the issues with her son. I already had my own theories floating around my head. Something told me that there had been a strain ever since Hayden's father died. But, I felt uncomfortable and it wasn't my place yet to question her about any of it.

"Thank you." I could have sworn she was trembling.

"You're welcomed, and you know what? Call me when you get back from Catalina. We'll have lunch before you go back to Santa Barbara." Hoping that somehow I could mend whatever was going on, I extended that invitation.

There is no way I could have predicted what would come next.

When I got into the car, Hayden took his glasses off and just stared at the steering wheel.

"Hayden, what happened back there, baby?"

"Nothing, besides my mother sticking her nose in places it doesn't belong. I don't want you getting too close to her because you'll end up with your feelings hurt."

"I think I can handle your mother."

Hayden was being unreasonable. Mareena had been great to me, so far. Surely he was just upset in the heat of the moment, and it would blow over.

We wouldn't discuss their issues until much later.

And then, there was HayLex

*T*here was pressure from all sides. Our families felt left out because we had eloped. As for the Press - they were worse. It had been almost a month since Hayden and I married, and the media felt ripped off. No pictures, no story - nothing. As Ok! magazine so boldly put it: *Hollywood playboy, Hayden Jones finally settles down with a nice girl - and left us all in the dark!*

People magazine's online blog devoted two pages to our relationship: *Alexia Diamond: Who is the unknown beauty who pinned down box office hunk, Hayden Jones?*

Then the inevitable – we were dubbed "HayLex" by the media. I didn't understand the big hoopla. But, it's like it gave hope to the masses of dreamers out there. There were internet celebrity fashion blogs that now included *Alexia Diamond's style.* They found photos of me pre-Hayden, and compared them to my present fashion choices. Some of it hurt my feelings and was way off base. I was a respected makeup artist and had access to high end designers long before Hayden Jones - thank you very much.

Hayden had married a "normal" girl and it was exciting to a lot of people. It wasn't like the Tom and

Katie level of craziness, but enough to make me very self-consciousness.

"Stacee, what do you think? Should we have a big party? You know, let a couple of magazines in on it, or whatever. Maybe then, they'll calm down."

"Girl, they're not going to leave you alone. You know they're calling you guys HayLex, right?" Stacee was amused.

"I heard."

"This is just the beginning. But, yeah, I think you should because it will give us all a chance to celebrate with you."

"So, who do you suggest to help? Will you?"

"No - that's why God created party planners, girlfriend!" She giggled. "They'll be clamoring to do this."

Listening to Stacee's insight, I felt like a lost tourist, with no idea what I was doing. Being a guest at a Hollywood party and being the guest of honor carried completely different levels of expectation. The burden was heavy and I knew there was no getting around it.

Hayden wasn't concerned in the least because he knew all he had to do was show up. I on the other hand, was going to be in the spotlight, and if I didn't do it right, I'd forever be seen in their eyes as the nobody who married Hayden Jones. I had to love on everyone and make our guests feel special. Make my own mark.

One thing was for sure – it had to represent all of the romance surrounding our relationship. Hayden swept me off my feet, and I didn't have to do anything to draw him in. I now realized *that's* what the public was interested in. A big star fell in love with a commoner. As rude as it sounds, that's exactly what people think when this happens.

We were the It Couple of the hour. Hayden would always say to me, "This never happened, until I married you." A celebrity couple is more exciting because it feeds the fantasy. People look at Will and Jada or Brad and Angelina and think, 'Living these perfect lives, there's no way they could be like us'. I have news for those believers.

The paparazzi followed me around town, even staked out my doctor appointments. Fans showed up at our gates, hoping to catch one of us leaving. They were hungry for anything. Sometimes, I would stop and chat for a minute on my way out, to try and let them know that, yes, we're real people.

They didn't buy it.

"Oh my god, tell Hayden we love him! Can I get a picture, Alexia? Your man is so freakin' hot!"

Those proclamations came from girls *and* guys.

They adored Hayden, and because of that, they now adored me.

HayLex – there was no escaping it.

Stacee forced me to call Kaz to find out who could help us with the event. It had to be unique and lavish, but not typical Hollywood because *we* weren't typical Hollywood. I also knew that if we allowed the world to peek in on our fairytale, the event had to be romantic and perfect.

~

Kaz, on speaker, rattled off a couple names of key celebrity planners. He also told me that I needed an assistant because his hands were full with Hayden.

"Besides, we're friends. I don't want to take orders from my girlfriend. You're my anti-Hollywood gal pal!"

"Thank God for that!"

I wasn't sure if I was as "anti" as he suggested, but I sure as hell didn't want to go down in flames as a crazy Wife Of.

I chose just the right planner. Let's call her … **Money's No Object**, because she got the job done, at *any* cost. I checked out her website and after reading testimonials, was convinced that her reputation was well deserved. **Money** had orchestrated the most fabulous weddings in town. She creates the fantasy. Even if some of them only lasts seventy days.

Money and I were instantly on the same page. For instance, I didn't want the party to take place in Los Angeles. The hotels were over saturated and nothing would be held secret. She got that.

"Oh, no, no, no, Beverly Hills is *not* on my list for you! I'm taking you to Wine Country, my darling."

And, that she did.

After three days of parading in and out of event venues throughout Santa Barbara, **Money** pulled the magic out of her hat.

"There's an elegant ocean front estate that I want you to see."

"Is it empty?"

What good would an abandoned estate do me? There's no glamour in that, I thought, nibbling on a scone in the outdoor café of the Biltmore.

"No, no, no… it's active." She removed her Chanel sunglasses. "The family is *very* private… but I think for just the right interest they would be willing to allow us in for a week." There was a hungry ambition in those wide, amber eyes of hers that told me **Money** would all but move those people out of the house herself, for the right price. "I did their daughter's wedding and it was divine."

Money was convincing and I was now intrigued

about this grand palace.

An hour later, we drove through the gates of the oceanfront estate. I had never seen anything like it in all of my life. I got out of the car and took in the perimeter view.

"Hayden is going to love this. Do whatever you have to, **Money**!"

"Oh, honey, this place is as good as yours. Let's meet them, shall we?"

Just like that, I had found the location for the party. Those are the advantages of being a Hollywood couple.

Next stop: the guest list. With the exception of Lilly and Stacee, there weren't many friends on my must have list. Most noteworthy, were certain ones I intentionally left off. If you have doubts about anything or anyone – follow that gut instinct.   That is my advice to you.

Runaway to State Street

*T*he Friday of our "I Do after-party" as we called it, I had my parents driven by limo to the oceanfront, Tuscan-style villa. Mareena's house was nearby, but of course, I wanted her to stay with all of us. Hayden and I planned it to be a special weekend for our family and friends; and especially our parents. We both realized we had some serious making up to do. Everybody knows that weddings are about the mothers, and we blew it. In my mind, anyways.

This was the first time our parents were all together. Anxiety set in about our mothers meeting for the first time. These women have strong personalities and my mother can cut you down with her tongue when she feels like you're getting out of line, or trying to over step her. Couple that with Mareena having a couple of cocktails in her. She's eccentric and has little restraint, and my mother will tell you like it is. I feared the combination was a recipe for disaster. Thankfully, my peacemaking father would be there to *try* and hold together a sense of sanity.

~

Hayden's roaming hands woke me far too early on

Saturday morning. There's nothing I've ever loved more than sleep, but there are sacrifices I'm willing to make. But, that willingness was short lived.

"Good morning, baby." His morning voice was sexy.

Lying on my stomach, curled up with the pillow, I rolled over. "Heyyy…" I smiled whenever I saw his eyes in the morning and it was like a dream all over again. "…picking up where we left off?"

He laughed me off, which I didn't find amusing. "Nope! You have to get up. There's someplace I want to take you."

Glancing over at the bedside clock, I thought I was seeing things. My head was throbbing from the bottomless martinis I stupidly consumed the night before. I dreaded leaving the huge custom California King with its overstuffed pillows and silk linens that **Money** had brought in for our stay. She coordinated everything to our liking.

"Hayden, it's too early for sightseeing."

Even so, I indulged him because Hayden didn't get excited over many things. Like the party. He said it was all for me. So, I wondered where on earth we were headed at seven in the morning.

State Street in Santa Barbara is something of a make believe scene straight out of a Rockwell photo. From the tree lined, cobblestone streets to clay tiled mission style buildings.

The family-owned café we arrived at had been a favorite of Hayden's for many years. We walked in and right away, a waitress nodded and greeted us with a smile and the man behind the counter came out and hugged Hayden.

"Welcome back, Hayden." He reminded me of Chevy Chase, and was just as jovial. "And, who is this lovely young lady?"

Hayden wrapped his arm around me. "I want you to meet my wife, Alexia."

"Oooh…and what a beautiful smile." The man clapped his hands together like he'd won a prize. "Welcome, my dear." He cupped my hand with his. "I'm Charles. You know, this guy is like family around here."

Charles was so kind, the way he made me feel at home.

The café was a warm, safe place and Hayden fit in like one of the locals. With celebrity checked at the door, he was a regular guy, bringing his wife to breakfast.

"Thank you. It's so nice to meet you. Your café is lovely, Charles. I already know that I'll be back." I meant every word.

"Of course, you will." He rushed over pulling a chair

out for me, while Hayden went to the deli counter, browsing over the delicacies.

"Alex, just wait until you taste the food. They'll make anything for you, right Charles?"

"Yes, yes, whatever you want!"

We sat in there enjoying Belgian waffles and organic teas for well over an hour. Hayden told me the story of how Santa Barbara had become his second home and that his mother stumbled across the café during a shopping visit years before. She brought him back there, and it's been a favorite ever since.

I hold dear the memory of first visiting Charles' magical little café on State Street - for more reasons than one.

If these cliffs could talk

&y early Saturday afternoon, the estate was a circus of activity. **Money's No Object** had arrived early that morning, dictating to her staff the final details of the party. While I was out in Santa Barbara with Hayden, she called me, frantic with questions.

"Look, **Money**… you've got this, okay? I completely trust your decision on those details."

"Well thank you."

"Besides, the only thing I care about is keeping nosey ass people out of that house."

I'd warned her that no guests other than immediate family were allowed into the main house. Not only because it wasn't our home, but Hayden was notorious for growing bored with guests real quick and would probably choose to abandon them to our own party inside. I had begun to understand his reactions far better than when we first met. And usually, the partygoers didn't much care, as long as the merrymaking kept on for them. Half of those on the list were curious space fillers anyways.

So at that moment, what **Money** was dealing with, was the last thing I cared about. We were paying *her* to sweat over whether pedals should line the pathway where we would enter.

You never know how these events will turn out, but trying to be optimistic, I had decided that the party was going to be fabulous, and it was. Our guests arrived at the villa in their finest formal duds. Everyone would finally be able to celebrate with us and share in our joy for a night. Romance was definitely in the air.

At just before seven o'clock I was trotting in my bare feet across the upstairs landing, holding up the flowing hem of my corseted, white Atelier Versace gown. I found my mother in one of the parlors.

"Mom? Oh – there you are! Only you will tell me the truth. Is this too much?"

She waved off the notion. "For an occasion like this, there's no such thing as too much." She adjusted the Neil Lane diamond brooch which held my hair back on one side. "You look so pretty, Alexia." I stood shocked that she didn't criticize me for not looking innocent enough. "Good thing you have small boobies, girl. The dress pushes you up, though."

And, there it was.

My mother couldn't deliver a clean compliment to me without slipping a little dagger in there. I took it, reasoning that she was still punishing me for running off and not letting her have that wedding she'd always dreamed of.

"Alright, well, I'm going to finish getting ready, so Hayden and I have a moment before everyone gets here."

I love my mother and would do just about anything for her, but she always finds some way of making me feel bad about myself. But, I let it go that night.

"Alexia, love….. are you ready?" **Money** looked around the great room with a perplexed look on her face. "Where is your husband? Your entrance is in two minutes, and…"

"And… he's right here." Hayden walked up behind me, with a hug, kissing my cheek."You're beautiful."

"Thank you, baby." I got a kick out of watching **Money's** pressure rise. *Loosen up, lady!* "I think **Money** thought you weren't coming." I teased at her expense.

"You two look amazing!"

That, we did. Hayden was wearing a black Versace tux. Head-to-toe Versace: our nod to the days when couples complimented each other in every way.

Money kept on. "Also, in addition to our photographer, I want to remind you that Beverly Hills Woman magazine is here." Scrolling through her phone **Money** gave the lowdown. "They will be photographing notable guests, the gorgeous decor, and of course…the two of you. But, it was made very clear by your assistant that the reporter is to in no way try and interview you or she will be escorted out."

"Good, thank you." Hayden was getting impatient and ready to get it rolling.

"Yes, we just want to have a good time with our family."

Tucking her phone into the pocket of the tight, pale pink, Chanel suit, **Money** escorted us out to the garden. It may not have been my wedding day, but it was the closest feeling I got to wedding day jitters.

As we entered the party tent, right on cue, DJ Milan, one of the most sought after music masters in the country, announced, "Ladies and Gentlemen, Mr. and Mrs. Hayden Jones…. Give it up!" I had never heard of him, but Hayden requested Milan and apparently he was booked at club LAX in Vegas the same night, but miraculously… he became available for us. Imagine that.

Everyone cheered and whistled, while camera flashes popped off around the room. I spotted Stacee right away, in an emerald green cut-out Azzedine Alaia evening gown. Her Plus-One was gorgeous, but unfamiliar to me. Hayden's long-time friend, Grammy winning superstar, Morgan Bryant and his new wife were in attendance, as he would perform later. And, then of course, Lilly and Jerzy were up front and center; all smiles. It would be a night to remember. After weeks of guilt and pent up nerves, I could finally party.

Money's No Object had outdone herself by bringing my vision to life. From the luxurious linens sweeping the ceiling of the tent, with crystal chandeliers that appeared to hang freely, to the exotic flowers and romantic table settings complete with ghost chairs...it was a dream.

We cut the cake after dinner, then DJ Milan kicked it up a notch and the dance floor was filled. Even good ol' Rusty Fisk let his hair down. I danced with him to one of Nelly's songs. Rusty was a little nervous, I could tell; like he might not be able to contain himself much longer, but feared Hayden canning his ass if he didn't stop reading my cleavage. Hayden sat in one of the lounge areas on the lawn, talking to actress Khloe Kimbers and her husband, who were our neighbors at the time, when he caught my attention and motioned behind him. I couldn't believe my eyes.

What the hell are they doing out there? Not tonight, you don't! I thanked Rusty for the dance and took off.

There was Lilly, in a breathtaking chiffon Dior dress, crying and screaming at Jerzy like a lunatic, just yards away from the cliff. If I didn't know any better, I would have sworn one of them was going over.

"Excuse us." Hayden cut me off at the pass, stopping me from running over to them. "Alex, don't get involved in their stupid shit." Rubbing my shoulders, he convinced me to stay away from them. "I don't want you upset. This is *our* night. They're just... here." We kissed, while I still heard echoes of Lilly's voice.

"Hold that. Perfect - You're such a beautiful couple!"

Just in the nick of time, the photographer caught a tender moment. Luckily, he missed me as I was poised to play referee for my dysfunctional friends. That shot, by the way, landed the cover story for Star magazine: *Hayden & Alexia: Inside their romantic wedding celebration.*

At the end of Morgan's dedication, Hayden and I thanked our guests and disappeared inside the villa to enjoy the rest of the evening our way. From the master suite we could see the flashing lights beyond the terrace, as the party revelers danced the night away.

"This isn't *anything* like LA." Staring out into the night, I didn't miss the demands of the Hollywood lights and glaring eyes.

"Maybe we'll find a house up here." Hayden leaned against my back, kissing my neck as he unzipped my gown. "But tonight, this place is ours." As he picked me up and carried me to the bed, I realized I had missed the over-the-threshold moment. This was it.

I longed for Hayden's touch. No man made me feel the way he did. Not before, and not since. When you love someone as deeply as I did him, feeling their breath against your skin, watching them enjoy your body, sends you into a euphoric state. The way he looked intensely into my eyes, unlike most men who selfishly closed their eyes. My response to his thrusts turned him on even more. My moans heightened with every stroke, filling me deeper, as he whispered in my ear how much he loved and needed me. I opened up every inch of my soul and handed it over to him. Hayden loved me and nothing else was important. We were lost in each other.

We had it all - Love, great sex and a lifestyle people envied. I almost felt sad for Lilly that night; she thought she was living the dream. To some extent, she was. But, I wondered what Jerzy had done to send her over the edge like that, because it was a far cry from her praises of him in my apartment a couple years back. Surely, I would find out soon.

But Boy... if those cliffs could talk.

Keeping it 100

*T*he Sizzling 100 celebration is legendary. Its paparazzi swarmed red carpet is always a colorful parade of gorgeous women, athletes and hip hop stars, sprinkled with undercover execu-perverts hoping for a little face time with some of the famous beauties on the list. I was commissioned as makeup artist for one of the night's celebrated bombshells.

Swimsuit model and actress, Sabrina Fortis was Number 7 on the list and I was recruited to her glam squad, making sure it was known that she deserved that spot. I was excited when Sabrina's agent called me to do her makeup for the event. I felt like everyone else had assumed I would now sit back and eat bon-bons on Rodeo Drive all day, because I had married a huge star. Well, I wanted just the opposite. A gig like this one was what I dreamed of back in Barstow. I was finally making a name for myself.

When I arrived at Sabrina's Londonberry Place home, above the Sunset Strip, I admit that I was surprised by the coziness of it all. From the unassuming gate, to the shabby chic décor, it was clear to me that she was a fairly down to earth girl. Who would have guessed?

Still I wondered, *why'd this girl ask for me?* Although, I was glad she did.

Opening the door, Sabrina was bubbly and very gracious as she welcomed me in.

"Oh my god, Alexia Diamond Jones, or... is it just Jones?"

"Either is okay...Hi, how are you?" I couldn't help but smile. Her giddiness was contagious.

"Cool, well thank you so much for being on board with this...." Shooing her puppy to stop sniffing around my Tory Burch sandals, she continued. "...it's just that sometimes, well... you get these nosey makeup artists who just want to snoop around for anything to gossip about later. I know *you* would have no reason to do that."

"You're right, and the pleasure is mine, Sabrina." Looking around I tried steering us back on track. "Your home is so pretty. It's like a breath of fresh air up here."

"Thanks! I get to live a pretty normal life, when I'm finished with all of that...out there." Tip-toeing down the hall, with her auburn locks swinging behind her, Sabrina led me to a room, where we would get started. There was only four hours before she had to be on the red carpet at The Pacific Design Center.

Her dressing room, full of racks of clothes and shoes,

was complete with a lit mirrored make up station, and across the hall, was her gym. Sabrina invested in herself, her product so to speak, and that's why she was one of the highest paid models of the year. She was no air-head.

I also enjoyed the fact that she was discrete, and wouldn't ask me a thousand questions about *my* private life. As I prepped, she did ask one, though.

"Are you going to keep taking clients, or…?"

It was clear what that meant. *Are you going to stop now that you married Hayden?*

It was the question I had asked myself a thousand times.

"I'm not sure, because there's a lot that I have to focus on right now, but I will say this… being here, right now…is a good feeling. Doing what I love."

"I'd heard that Hayden Jones had married a makeup artist, and not some so-called starlet. Embarrassed to say, I looked you up online and wanted to work with you."

"You didn't!" That was the funniest thing I'd heard in a while.

"Oh yes I did, and my manager called Lorena Maldono to find you."

There was hope that I would keep working, but

things were different now. I wasn't sure how Hayden felt about my career, or even the fact that I had one. Did he view it as serious or something I enjoyed while I *had* to do it?

When I told him about working with Sabrina, he *claimed* to not know who she was. Then declared: "You know you don't have to do that, right, babe?" He made it sound so insignificant.

"I know I don't but I want to. Sabrina's a top model and she asked for me. This feels good for me, to be taken seriously as an artist."

"I'm sorry, you're right, it is." He hugged me because he saw he had hit a nerve. "Have a good time."

"Hayden, it's work - not a party!"

Hayden was so insensitive sometimes. I knew right then, he saw it as a hobby. But one thing I was determined about... I would not let him blot out my goals. I had worked too hard to get where I was.

I finished applying the glossy, crimson lip color just as Sabrina's manager rang the doorbell. She had one of the sexiest faces I had ever seen. Good cheeks, fabulous brows and naturally full lips.

"I love it! You're so good, Alexia." She swirled the chair around, and with a serious tone, confessed, "I just want to say this... I know what it's like to be married to someone who sweeps you off your feet and takes care of everything." She told me about getting married at twenty-three years old in Miami and how her soon-to-be ex-husband, a respected dentist in Bal Harbour, treated her like a princess but demanded she stay at home. Like his trophy. She sank deeper and deeper into herself, before finally running away one night. "Don't let that happen to you, okay?"

All I could do was gaze at her and smile. "Okay." It was awkward but her words hit deep.

Every time I see a Sports Illustrated swimsuit cover or commercial featuring Sabrina, what she told me that day, echoes in my head. So many times, a woman gets lost in the shadow of her husband.

I hoped that would never apply to me.

Drunken Confessions

It was raining buckets when I returned home from the Women of Style luncheon at the Montage in Beverly Hills. That meant I was dressed to the nines and had on fabulous shoes, which I did not want to get ruined.

Focusing on getting inside the garage, I drove right past the car parked along the hedges. Shaking my umbrella off is when I noticed the white, older E-Class Mercedes. I wondered who it belonged to.

There was an unfamiliar voice as I walked towards the media room at the far end of the house. It was either one of Hayden's friends or someone he didn't want seen. The media room was a place industry folks were rarely invited to. It was Hayden's personal space – off limits to "the business".

Knocking, I kept in. "There you are." A slightly pudgy man, with an awful toupee craned his neck around. "Oh, I'm interrupting."

"No, it's alright." Hayden stood up, rubbing his chin. A self-conscious habit of his I had long picked up on. "Dr. Bob… my wife, Alexia Jones."

"It's nice to meet you. I think." *What kind of doctor?*

"Is… everything okay?" A script of possibilities ran through my overworked mind.

"It's a pleasure, Mrs. Jones. Yes…We're about finished here." He said, looking at Hayden for confirmation.

It was then that I concluded he was a psychiatrist of some sort.

Excusing myself, I went upstairs to avoid any secret handshakes that might occur for my sake. While I was frowning over the rain spots on my Alberta Ferretti skirt, Hayden walked into the bedroom. I wondered why that man had been there.

"Hey… are you okay?" I removed the skirt, tossing it on a chair. "Why was the doctor here, sweetie?"

"Yeah, I uh… just needed to talk through some things."

"Right, well you can talk to me, too."

"You don't need to deal with this stuff."

I had no clue as to where this was coming from, so I hugged him. "Try me." I wanted him to know I had his back in everything. "I love you and will always be on your side, no matter what."

Hayden sighed and tightened his arms around me. "That's one thing I do know."

"Good…"

I put together a big salad, while steaks were being delivered from Spago. Who knew Wolfgang Puck delivered? We opened up a bottle of wine and ate on the covered patio, like we did on our first date. The clouds were heavy and the lights of neighboring properties over the hills were just barely visible. The smell of the rain was so soothing. I hoped Hayden could relax and fill me in, because I could tell he was dealing with something heavy.

"I had a good day today. Met some really fascinating women; the grand dames of Bel Air and Beverly Hills, you know how that goes."

"Right, I remember you telling me about that." Lying back on the chaise, Hayden peering into the glass as he sipped, I could tell we were in different places. "And, what happened?"

"Well, there was fashion show and silent auction. Oh! By the way, I won the bid on a vintage Chanel bag. They *claim* Coco designed it herself."

Hayden nodded, without so much of a glance at me. "I'm sure it's nice."

"It cost you a pretty penny, too." Catching on that he wasn't in a joking mood, I asked, "What's going on with you, and why was this Dr. Bob here?"

"To remind me that I'm not my father." At that, he finally looked up. The candlelight shone in his eyes.

"What do you mean?" I pulled my legs up, reclining on the sofa.

"When you pretend for a living, it can… cause problems. Sometimes the lines become blurred."

I didn't know what to say, except throw in an "I know…" I was trying to understand.

"You can't always be yourself, so most of the time you stay in pretend mode, just to feel comfortable." He seemed resentful of that. "I was biking up Mulholland today, and thought about how my father worked so hard and was almost never home, earning a living for us … building the dream. Then, he got sick…" Hayden reached over and opened a second bottle. "Try this Pinot Noir, it's amazing." He poured some for me. "…and he died." He flicked the bottle cork across the patio.

My heart ached for Hayden. He was still hurting over losing his father.

"I know baby, but… he did it all to give you what he never had. Your mother always talks about how much he loved you."

"He did, I know that. But, it's funny that she tells you that, when she almost blames him for getting sick and suggests that the same will happen to me. Yet, she doesn't turn anything down."

"No, I'm sure she doesn't mean it like that." Inside, I

wasn't sure of anything.

"She says, 'Hayden you work too much, making all of this money. Your father was the same way.' Like I'm going to work myself to the grave, the way she drove him to."

I sat up. "Oh, Hayden, don't say that."

"It's true, Alex. My mother makes me crazy. You don't know her." He finished off the second bottle.

"Okay… let me fill you in on something."

"Here we go…What?"

"I'm serious, Hayden… listen. You know how critical my own mother is of me. It's been like that since I was a little girl. I used to write goodbye notes to her. I never gave them to her, but I filled those notes with reasons why I wanted to get as far away as possible. That's when I knew I would leave to go to Los Angeles. I knew it when I was a teenager. Go and be someone else. My father always stood up for me like he still does." Like an idiot, I started crying. "He paid for my apartment when I first came here, did you know that?"

"I'm sorry, Alexia, I didn't mean to…"

"It's okay. The point is – we don't have to live for our parents; the way they want us to. Look at you - you became Hayden Jones, for God's sake!" Hayden chuckled under his breath at my ramblings. "You know what I mean."

The rain held steady, but we were seemingly oblivious to it. Hayden and I spent hours sharing stories of sneaking out of the house as teenagers, having our hearts broken and all of the moral sacrifices we made to get what we wanted, which probably leads to why neither of us really trusts anyone.

We held a confessional over three bottles of wine.

"Hold that thought - we need more, babe." I got up and ran into the house.

With calculated steps, I wobbled back outside, plopping down onto the deep seated sofa waving a bottle of Fireball. We drank from the bottle, like pros. By the time that night was over, we had washed our pathetic memories away.

My head was cloudy in the morning, as I woke up just before Noon, on top of the made bed, in only my panties and Jimmy Choo wedge sandals. Hayden laid dead asleep, jeans on, but undone, like he had made a failed attempt at undressing. We were trashed. I peeked outside the bedroom door and immediately saw a trail of clothes, including my dress, bra and Hayden's shirt and shoes, leading from the staircase, and down the hall to our door. I'm sure Sylvie had walked past that shameful display and left it there, as a reminder.

That was the first sloppy drunk night of my life.

Unfortunately, it would not be the last.

One thing I clearly remember was Hayden saying he had never trusted anyone the way he did me. It's like we were equals in all of our inner torment and insecurities. A match made in Hollywood Heaven.

Supreme Defiance

"You'll get the hang of this really quick, Alex!"

Kaz sat across from me in the limo, giving me a rundown of how it goes at a movie premier.

Hayden chimed in. "It's a cakewalk. The whole thing lasts like, 10 minutes. Just keep smiling and have fun. They'll love you."

Hayden was especially good at making me feel like I was the center of his universe. Everyone else was just lucky enough to share our world. In the meantime, I knew waiting for me were more metaphorical magnifying glasses and judgmental specs. *Where did he find this one? Why'd he marry her so quickly? – Ah, she's pregnant – that's it!*

It was the Labor Day weekend premier of Hayden's long awaited high octane film, Supreme Defiance. This night needed to be perfect.

Sitting in the back of the limo, I felt like I was sweating something awful. Hayden was the star, but the heat would be on me as his latest trophy. That's how the media projected us.

Hayden was show stopping in the navy colored custom tailored Gucci suit, with his signature white tee underneath, paired with Gucci loafers. The fashion stylist hit the mark with that look. And, best of all, the ensemble was a freebie from the Rodeo Drive boutique. One of the biggest perks of celebrity life - all of the free clothes we receive just to parade around town in high-style designer duds. You become walking billboards. When it goes on record that Hayden Jones rocked the latest Gucci couture, the sales skyrocket, big time.

I desired a more subtle, yet tempting look. The winner for the night was a metallic Stella McCartney thigh length dress which showed nothing but my toned legs and Gucci steel-heeled stilettos. A sexy distraction would surely work in my favor amongst the glaring eyes.

"That's easier said than done, Hayden. You already know they love *you*."

His face scrunched as he clarified my statement. "Alex, these people don't love me, come on... They love the characters I bring to the screen. They don't know us, and I like to keep it that way. But, I give 'em what they pay for." He peered ahead out the window as we approached the theater. "Hollywood is mostly bullshit. Remember that."

I wondered how he did it day in and day out, if he *really* felt that way.

I laughed, "Okay, I'll try."

Rusty Fisk turned around from the front seat, talking at and giving orders to us like we were his kids. "You know the drill Hayden. You ready?" His hooded eyes then cut to me. "Alexia, it gets wild out there, but you stick with me. It'll be…"

"No, I want my wife right by my side." Hayden demanded, as his hand rested on my thigh, which sent a crazy chill across my body.

"Thank you, baby. " Reaching my arm around his, I leaned my head on his shoulder. "I'm so proud of you."

I was ecstatic that Hayden spoke up to his manager, because I was about to tell that little man to shove his bossy ways right up his ass.

Rusty glared at me like he wanted to wish me into oblivion. "Yeah, fine. Whatever… I mean, that's even better. Alright, we're here."

We finally arrived at the El Capitan Theater. The driver opened the door and Hayden got out first, to the wave of screams. As he helped me out and I stepped onto Hollywood Boulevard, I looked down at my foot where the edge of the red carpet started. It was like an out-of-body experience.

There I was, my first time walking the red carpet with my movie star husband. *That first hit - it's the greatest high, and you can never get it back.* As I tell you now, it felt amazing and I soaked it all in.

Giant Supreme Defiance posters were plastered along the barricades and the red carpet. I looked up at the image of Hayden, in military fatigues, holding a high-powered weapon, reigning above the entrance of the theater. "This is crazy!" I felt drunk by it all.

The paparazzi were in force behind the barricades along the carpet and the flashes were blinding.

"This is my wife, Alexia. She's gorgeous, isn't she?" Hayden proudly introduced me to the press. I found it strange, but loved it at the same time, as I posed and waved at the fans, who were yelling towards us.

The two of us posed together, him with his co-stars and then Hayden alone. All of a sudden I looked up and he was running across the street towards throngs of fans, now going bonkers behind barricades. He posed for pictures and signed autographs. I couldn't help but laugh because it was like Hayden became a different person with his fans. He was so alive. What Hayden described in the limo, no longer applied.

Kaz quickly ran behind Hayden to help navigate the situation. The security guards couldn't keep up, so they finally ushered him back towards the theater.

I playfully poked at his ribs, "You were wrong, Hayden. The fans *do* love you!"

He grinned. "This is when being in this business is fun; meeting the fans."His eyes smiled and I loved it.

"I see that."

We made our way inside after a few minutes of meeting and greeting, shaking hands and all of the formalities. There was a barrage of celebrities on the red carpet, all dressed up for the photo ops. I wondered which ones would end up ripped to shreds in the celebrity blogs the next day. The whole time praying that those same writers would take it easy on me; being my first major public appearance and all.

~

Okay - I didn't care for the film.

Supreme Defiance is not what I normally choose when going to the movies. It was violent and bloody and full of more F-bombs than I could keep up with. It was all of the stuff that Hayden's twenty million-per-picture salary counted on. Supreme Defiance would go on to be a box office smash, of course, as he continued to reign as one of Hollywood's top draws.

Hayden could tell I didn't enjoy the film. No matter how proud I was of him, or how huge my smiles were at the premier, I did a lousy job at hiding that fact.

"So tell me what you hated about the film, Alex."
Hayden turned towards me in the backseat of the limo,
on our way to a private production party at the
Hollywood Roosevelt. After a few seconds of me
struggling to come up with the right words, he stepped
to my rescue, "It's okay, baby. You're not obligated to
love everything I do. As long as I know I can count on
you to have my back when it counts, it's all good." He
smiled, while still waiting for my response.

I snuggled closer to him, hoping that would ease the
blow because I didn't want to hurt his feelings. Not that
I really could. "You were incredible, sweetie! You
were... it's just... you know I still can't get used to some
of the effects. The audience loved it. They couldn't stop
shouting at the end. You saw!" Almost embarrassed by
my eager persistence to please him, I poured myself a
glass of champagne. "You want some? Let's celebrate,
huh?" I spilled some on my YSL clutch. "Dammit!"

Hayden gave me a squeeze and a kiss, which I'm
sure he knew, would calm me down. "Babe, what's
really wrong?"

"I don't know. This whole thing hit me tonight. I'm
just a little antsy about what they all think of me."

"Don't worry about the press or the fans." He held
his phone up. "Here... let's give 'em something."
Hayden snapped a pick of us in an embrace and posted

it to social media pages with the caption *My wife – trying to rip my clothes off in the back of this limo!*

One Selfie later, I had thousands of curiosity seekers and more followers all in my business.

As we entered the Roosevelt lobby I spotted a familiar face right away. I tried to ignore her. *Trash from the past*, I thought.

E! News and Access Hollywood were covering the event and I recognized **Pretty Reporter** right away, when she popped up in front of us as soon as we walked in. All the while, Hayden held me tight as if I was his prized possession. I didn't mind. It felt good to be by his side, and because I was feeling so insecure already, I hoped he didn't find her attractive. None of the people around me were my friends. Hayden was the one I trusted with my whole being. So, attached to him is where I wanted to be.

I was surprised when the reporter acknowledged me, shoving the mic in my face, asking how I enjoyed the film.

"How are you, Alexia? You look stunning."

"I'm good, thank you."

"Did you enjoy the film? The critics are saying Supreme Defiance will be the smash hit of the holiday weekend."

"Oh, I loved it. I mean, it's my man up there doing his thing, you know? I'm very proud, of course!"

I smiled, turning away from cameras that were inches from being down my throat - putting me on the spot. **Pretty Reporter** wasn't impressed with me or my answer, but I didn't really care. If it weren't for the drink I had on the way over, I don't know how I would have responded - or *if* I could have, for that matter. This was Hayden's territory, not mine.

I still loved seeing Hayden on the big screen. Thinking how gorgeous he always looked and that the guy who was everyone's on-screen hero, was the love of my life. I was on cloud nine.

That's until that whore from the past intentionally side-swiped me.

"Hello darling, look at you, Alexiaaaa…" Monet Caprice's fake accent swam through the air of the Roosevelt hotel that night like the stench of a cheap hooker's perfume.

"Oh, hi, how are you? Long time…" I was recounting the reasons why I stopped calling her.

It had been ages since I'd seen Monet. I heard from Lilly that she had conned her way onto that guess-which-one game show as a hostess and traded up apartments, as she now had a condo in the Sierra Towers in West Hollywood. On some foreign business man's dime, no less. It's tough being an "actress" in Hollywood.

Double kisses and mutual cringes were exchanged. Inside of me stirred an uneasy feeling about how she was at the party, and even worse, *why* she was there. It wasn't to catch up on girl talk with me. I'm surprised she even spoke to me, since the last time we saw each other… I kicked her out of my apartment.

"Monet", or Monica, which is her real name, came banging on my door close to Midnight. It was around the time I had started dating Hayden. She had no idea about him, but this idiot was practically kicking my door down. I opened it, and she lit into me with fury in her eyes.

"Who in the hell do you think you are spreading these lies about me?"

"Get your ass out of here, Monet!"

"Exactly, and don't you forget it!" She turned and stormed off.

I could hear her door slam with no regard for anyone else, at that hour.

Monet was furious because I had unraveled her big lie. It's okay for someone to create a new life for themselves. Sometimes a new persona is what's needed. But – don't use other people to help you look top-notch when you're nothing but a polished up tramp.

I had thrown some things out in the dumpster. An old rug, some designer shoes I no longer wore because they had scuffs, along with some old bottles of Dom and Moet that I used to line the top of my kitchen cabinet with. Well – I was hanging out with Monet one night and realized not only did we share taste in champagne, but her rug looked very familiar.

I didn't ask her about it. But, I may have mentioned it to Rob and Sam, the guys from downstairs. Hence, word getting back to Monet. Those gossip queens couldn't wait to call her out.

That was the last time we spoke. Monet avoided me like the plague ever since. Until now.

Monet ran her skinny fingers across her blunt bangs and quickly glanced at Hayden, then past him, without so much of a Hello or Congratulations. I knew that bitch was trying to make me feel threatened. Hayden seemed to intentionally ignore her, then kissed my cheek and walked off with his manager, quicker than I could receive it.

"I know, girl... and look at you now. You two are the talk of this town. Hayden is a lucky man." Nodding her head, she gulped back a glass of champagne; more than likely her second or third. "Ummm, hmmm... I tell you..." Monet's heavily lined eyes peered into mine, with a smirk on her face, like she was dying to get back at me. She looked around. "I'd better find my gentleman." She leaned in whispering, while her new breasts spilled from the black sequined Leger dress she was wearing. "Producer types - you know how they get."

I wanted to kick her. "Not really. Okay... well, good to see you. Let's have lunch and catch up, yes?"

Half-hugging Monet, I broke free before I asked to see her black book. Mostly because I feared what I might find in it. I couldn't have gotten away from her quick enough.

Dumpster-diving slut.

First stop, Mr. Chows

From the beginning something I knew about Hayden was that he loved being a celebrity. He didn't duck and dodge the cameras as much as some celebs around town pretended to. He flirted with the fact that people wanted to know what he was up to. There was now even a celebrity blog section called *Keeping up with the Joneses*. Hayden's social media fan pages were full of photos of the two of us. Everyone had something to say about Alexia Diamond. Whenever I mentioned it to Hayden, he would just say, "Why are you so wound up about them? You should worry when they stop caring."

So either I could drown in this fish bowl or allow them to get to know a bit more of me, from a distance. I pondered it back and forth. I had thrived on hanging out with celebrities before I met Hayden, which is why I initially wanted to meet him. I admit it: I was the ultimate Hollywood girl. Always jumping on invites to rub shoulders and link myself to the Who's Who of Hollywood.

Now, it was me in the glass bubble and I hated it. Still, I used that power to feed them in hopes they would eventually back off. Especially when Hayden and I had kids, the paparazzi would have to stop, you would think.

So the cat and mouse game began. Sometimes, I initiated a day-to-day *Where's Alexia?* hunt: calling ahead at restaurants, making reservations for Lilly and me, under Hayden's name, and then my favorite - driving around in the Range Rover instead of my own car. Everyone recognized his ride. The attention was even arousing while it lasted. *They'll get sick of me soon enough.*

One night I'd made plans with Lilly and decided that if they wanted to see, I'd show them. I suggested we go to Mr. Chow's. Now, everyone in Hollywood knows that if you want to end up in the tabs, just show up at Mr. Chows and the pack of wolves would be scrambling at the curb to snap that first naked leg stepping out of the car.

We didn't disappoint. Lilly and I collaborated to look as irresistible as possible. She in a deep pink, one-shoulder David Meister dress, which I'm now convinced she had a direct hookup to his show room because she apparently had a closet full. I decided on all black Lanvin – a booty-hugging pencil skirt and sleeveless lace top. "Dress to make them squirm and send them home to finish off." Was what Lilly said. Not sure about being some sweaty guy's visual aid, I just wanted to give them something to gawk over and put in the press. Show them that Alexia does have style, after all.

Hayden knew what I was up to and he was fine with it because he was all about showing me off. Besides, he's the one who told me, "If you push back too much, they won't be there when you need them." Little did he know that one day, those very words would be on my side. Funny guy, my husband was.

Our limo cruised up Rodeo Drive and you could see all of the tourists with their cameras slung across their shoulders. The shadowy flashes popping off at Via Rodeo looked creepy at night. It felt like *Them versus Us*.

"Why are these people walking around taking a thousand pictures? They should just enjoy the moment. Beverly Hills is so beautiful at night." Lilly had definitely evolved into one of the Us; the kind that I didn't want to be. She shook her head, running her hands through her honey locks, showing off the chocolate diamond bracelet and the matching ring on her right hand. "It seems like yesterday that we were party girls roaming these slums of Beverly Hills, and look at us now. Doesn't seem fair to be so happy, does it?"

Was she convincing herself?

The tone in Lilly's voice was ridiculously cynical. Giving a dead stare into my eyes, she sloppily drank back her glass of wine. I didn't know what was going on in her head, but it looked like a downward spiral.

"Save some for later, hon." Hearing my suggestion, she shrugged her shoulders and put the glass in a holder. I felt uncomfortable and called Hayden. "Hey…" That's all I could muster up, but he could hear in my voice that I wasn't feeling whatever was happening around me.

"Alexia?"

Hearing his voice separated me from Lilly's antics.

"Yeah?"

"After dinner, there's somewhere I want to take you."

"Really?"

My face must have perked up because Lilly had the nerve to mouth *What?*

Hayden was in one of his moods, which meant he was ready to play some sort of wait-and-see game. I wanted so badly to tell the driver to take me back home, right then.

"You'll enjoy it. I'll text you at ten." I checked my Cartier, it was almost eight. "Leave then, and have the driver bring you home first."

"I will. Bye." Obediently, I couldn't wait to follow his lead in the mysterious romp.

Mr. Chows was the first stop of what would be an

intriguing night. I was bored and it wasn't Lilly's fault. Selfishly though, I felt completely distant from her. My mind was someplace else.

Whatever Lilly was dealing with had nothing to do with my life.

I longed to be with Hayden.

Secret gardens and
the gourmet cookie

$\mathcal{S}$ome loves are so passionate that you need to come up for air, catch your breath, just long enough to submerge and experience the rush all over again.

That was Hayden and me.

We were so high off each other that we couldn't measure when too much was too much. That should have been a red flag.

There were times when the intensity was too much for the people around us to deal with. We were so into each other, that it was even suggested by the tabloids that we were faking it. Early on in our relationship, when Hayden slightly flirted with other women in front of me, I didn't feel threatened, because they didn't come close to what I gave him. I was secure in that Hayden desired everything about me and that I had a consuming hold on him. "The gourmet cookie" is how he described it. I giggle at that because I know some women would find it demeaning knowing her husband is obsessed with having sex with her. Not me. Often, I encouraged it.

At the break of dawn one morning, just after our first anniversary, and he having finished shooting all night, I picked Hayden up from Paramax Studios lot in a flaming red Maserati and we took off up the coast with no destination in mind. We exited at the first remotely interesting town that we could find, and checked into some little inn that had around ten rooms, and looked like it was out of one of those ghost town westerns. Having no idea where we were and not really concerned, we made love until we tired of seeing those walls. We checked out and kept up the coast until we arrived in Santa Barbara where we hid out for three days at the Montecito Inn.

It was a turn on to make love somewhere completely unrelated to our everyday life. I was motivated to do whatever and become whomever he wanted me to - and was willing - because it made the sex that much hotter. That's when Hayden discovered I was spontaneous and crazy enough for his games.

After dinner at Mr. Chows that night, the limo arrived at my house just before ten-thirty.

"I'm glad we did this Lilly. Just like old times, right?"

"Pretty close." She smiled, scrolling through the phone with her legs curled up on the seat.

"Yeah… Alright well, call me tomorrow."

Finally putting her phone down, she reached her arms out to hug me. "I will. Love you."

"Love you too, girlie." Scooting out of the limo, I

told the driver, "Please walk her to her door when you get there, would you?"

"Alex, I'm fine." Like a drunken child fanning me off, Lilly ordered the driver, "Let's go!" I slammed the door closed.

The limo disappeared out the gate and as I turned to walk up the lit walkway towards the house, Hayden opened the door.

"You were waiting for me?" I was intrigued.

"Not really." He grinned. "Are you ready?"

"Sure." I looked him up and down, beaming with curiosity. "Where are we going?"

"Someplace we can be ourselves."

He gave me a quick peck on my lips and pulled the door closed behind him, then kept towards the Mercedes S-550 parked in the circle. Dealers would often let Hayden test drive their cars for a month or so, in hopes that he would end up purchasing one. He hated when his cars became too recognizable.

"Hmmm, you got a new ride to play with, huh?"

"No, but you do." He handed me the keys.

"Oh my God, it's mine?" We had driven past the dealership the day before, and I playfully pointed the car out in the showroom window. "This is the one I wanted; the platinum color and everything!"

He got the Mercedes for me, just because I admired it from a distance.

Hayden just smirked at me. "As fine as you look right now we can't show up in anything less."

"And, don't you forget it." I giggled, snatching the keys from his hand. "I'm driving!" Settling into the fine interior, I felt I had seriously arrived.

He climbed in the passenger side. "Besides, we have to play it all out Alex, so that you really understand what our life is."

Hayden was talking in some mysterious code and I couldn't wait to get to the next point.

"Thank you, baby. I love you so much."

Hayden spoiled me, and I loved every bit of it.

When we arrived in Downtown Los Angeles, the streets were busy. It was eleven on a Saturday night and lines to the clubs were wrapped around the block. I thought *No way he is taking me to some nightclub.*

"Turn here."

I realized it was no Joe Blow nightspot when we pulled into an alley between a brick building I didn't recognize, and the parking garage next to it. The Westin Bonaventure hotel watched over us from the sky-high distance.

I looked around. The surroundings were a little suspect. "Where are we, Hayden?"

"Hold on a second." Checking the rear view mirror, Hayden made sure we weren't tailed. We weren't. There were just some revelers staggering past the alley off Figueroa Avenue. That's when the valet attendant come rushing out of nowhere to open my door.

"Good evening, Ma'am. How are you?" He was a good looking guy, around mid-twenties with an accent I couldn't place.

"Thank you. I'm good – how are you?"

"I'm well, thank you." When Hayden got out, the valet recognized him. "Welcome back, Sir." He robotically announced, "If you will so graciously leave any electronics with the hostess. Your vehicle will be waiting when you return."

I had no idea what was going on, but it felt weird.

Clutching my hand, Hayden picked up the pace, practically rushing me inside the mirrored door. "Thank you, my man!"

Once inside I was pleasantly shocked. The place looked more like a luxury hotel lobby, but the winding staircase told me that something much more exciting was ahead.

"Good evening, Mr. Jones." The young woman acknowledged me with a smile. "Mrs. Jones, welcome to the SoWest Club." The plastic looking, but pretty girl clad in a tailored silk embroidered dress, took the metallic gold card from Hayden's hands and swiped it. "Enjoy your evening."

During a swift elevator ride up those fourteen floors, I had a lot of questions, but decided to hold off. Still I thought *I saw no one milling around in that lobby and there was a card swipe.* The light bulb went off. "Wait – this is one of those places, isn't it?"

"What places?" Hayden watched the digital numbers count up to the penthouse floor.

"A kind of secret club, right?" I was getting more curious, and then whispered, as if someone was listening. "It's not a sex club, is it?"

"Do you wish it were?" Hayden laughed under his breath, pulling me close and whispered, "We go *there* next time."

"Stop." I blushed.

He looked down at me, "Everyone here is a part of our world, Alex. You can do what you want away from prying eyes." There was melancholy in his voice, like he needed to run away to secret places just to be free.

"Alright..." I stared at him as crazy visuals swam through my head. I had never experienced anything like that, first hand. The anticipation alone was titillating.

The elevator opened and ahead was the most gorgeous night view of the Los Angeles skyline I had ever laid eyes on. I stumbled in my Choos getting off the elevator because I couldn't wait. What was so amazing was that I immediately felt at home. *No one back in Barstow would ever believe this exists* I thought.

Once off the elevator, you were met by plush sofas and club chairs which sectioned off areas throughout the ornate room. The perimeter was completely glass. The mind-blowing view definitely set the tone.

"Hayden, this is incredible." I turned around to ask more questions, when I saw a very familiar man approaching, and greeting Hayden with a handshake. "Oh, hello." Trying to hold my composure (because this was surprise overload), I pulled my jaw up.

"Tate, you haven't met my wife, Alexia." Hayden smiled with pride in voice as he introduced me to actor Tate Bradley, who according to People magazine was The Sexiest Man Alive.

"Alexia, I'm glad to meet you. I'm Tate..." We double cheek kissed which was the norm.

"It's so nice to meet you, Tate."

Another out-of-body moment. There I was, at the virtual club house for movie star hunks, one of which was my husband. That could be too much for any girl to keep her sanity. Hayden had to have known what he was doing to me, and he probably was entertained by it all.

"I hope you know what you've gotten yourself into, marrying this guy." The two of them chuckled. I could see they were pretty good friends. Their interaction was fraternal, which I enjoyed. "I'm sorry I missed your wedding celebration. I was on location in India, but I heard it was fantastic." Tate has a Texas drawl that could lullaby you to sleep.

"Yes it was, and thank you so much for the gift. That was so sweet."

"My pleasure... Hayden, we're starting up in about fifteen, man." Tate excused himself and nodded at me, "Alexia..."

"He seems really nice." I couldn't stop smiling.

"Yeah, Tate is a good dude."

We walked down a long hallway that led outside, to a rooftop Zen garden. Wouldn't you know - just then a flighty and busty brunette scampered up to us with a half empty drink in her hand.

"Hayden, oh my god - did you see Tate, yet? They were waiting on you to get here." She then in her southern drawl, acknowledged me, "Hey, I'm Lorel... Lorel Kanyun."

"Wow, really?" *Stripper name if I'd ever heard one.* She obviously was quite familiar with Hayden. "I'm Alexia." An awkward few seconds passed while I smiled at

Lorel, and stood there, waiting for my husband to say something.

Hayden had been looking past her, into the garden but then woke up. "Lorel, meet my wife, Alexia." I watched him to sense if he seemed uncomfortable. He didn't. For some reason, that put me at ease.

She clasped her hands and then reached out grabbing my forearms. "Oh my god, that's great! You are so pretty and Hayden here is a doll. But, you know that already!" She smiled, giggled and talked and giggled some more. "Well I'm about to refresh this drink, but Alexia let's talk later while the boys play their little poker game."

"Sure, why not? I would love that."

I was interested in knowing more about Lorel Kanyun and what she brought to the table. Though I was sure that this girl had not been screwing my husband, I knew that her kind didn't hang around A-list celebrities for no reason. Let alone, be welcomed into the circle the way she was.

Off she went, strutting in her gold stilettos and backless halter jumpsuit I'd just seen in the Valentino boutique. She had good taste I give her that – porn name or not.

Hayden was quick to tell me that Lorel was Tate's

occasional girlfriend who had moved to Los Angeles from Dallas. It was common knowledge that Tate Bradley had enjoyed the company of an adult entertainer or two. I wanted to give her the benefit of doubt, but I'm sure Lorel fell into that category in some form.

Something about her reminded me of Monet Caprice: a cut-throat hustler. Only Lorel seemed like a what-you-see-is-what-you-get kind of gal. Not a fraud like that Monet. Lorel had huge boobs and an elegant enough face to be accepted into certain A-list circles. All you have to do is dress them up in designer digs and they slide right in. When it comes to these celebrity ornaments, you try to keep them close. That's how you keep them away from your man. Lorel Kanyun was ditzy enough to chat the night away and fill in all the blanks. I just needed to get it through to her that my eyes were wide open and she shouldn't bother thinking I'm completely clueless.

Around Midnight, a hostess wearing a mesh dress that fit her like a second skin brought over a plate of fancy snacks and Lemondrop martinis to wash them down.

"Can I bring you ladies anything else?" She was our dedicated hostess. The staff at the SoWest Club is assigned to specific VIPs for the evening. This young woman was very professional and I could tell she took every inch of her job seriously.

"I think I'm okay. How about you, Lorel?" I wondered where Hayden was because I was getting bored.

"I'm just fine, darlin'." She then glanced up at the hostess, flashing her Colgate smile. "We're good, but um…stick around for a while, just in case."

"Of course…" Pretty Miss Hostess slyly grinned in response and sashayed away.

"These girls around here are so efficient. Sometimes you get to take one home with ya." I wondered if Lorel was trying to shock me. Giggling at the surprised expression on my face, Lorel curled her feet up in the plush couch we sat on across from the windows. The atmosphere was intoxicating. "So… do you have *any* idea what goes down at these poker games?"

I sat at the other end of the couch, swinging my crossed leg over the edge while enjoying my drink. "Not really, because I'm not that interested in it… at all."

Rolling her eyes in laughter, Lorel couldn't wait to clue me in. "Well, girl let me show you!" She hopped to her feet, gesturing me with head motions. "Follow me. Bring your drink. Come on, now!"

Walking through the garden I caught glances from

some famous faces that I never even thought would know how to let their hair down. Much less know about a place like SoWest.

The grand wooden doors ahead of us read like a Do Not Enter sign. It was obvious to me not to open them, but Lorel turned one of the handles and surprisingly it was not locked. I felt like I was spying but then it dawned on me – *my* husband is a member. This girl was a step above a groupie and had the balls to overstep all kinds of boundaries. I wondered what more there was to her story and why she seemed to *know* it was okay for her to do all of this.

Her whispers delivered like shouts. "And, there they are. Come on, take a look."

I frowned because this chick was way out of line, but in my curiosity, I slid past her, peeking through the opening in the doors. I could smell the cigars, saw a half-naked red head handing out drinks, and then almost choked seeing the stacks of cash in the middle of the table. Not crumpled piles, but banded wads of bills. I tilted my head to get a better visual just as Hayden slammed his cards down in frustration. "Dammit, man! You just cost me ten grand!" I recognized the superhero he was blaming; or rather the actor who portrayed one on screen.

It was exciting, but felt wrong so I backed up, quietly

pulling the doors closed.

"Oh, whatever! They're big boys." I finished my drink off.

"True, but the money they waste, I could have a yacht by now. Tate will be in a bad mood for a week over this. He's a horrible player and keeps coming back for more whippings."

Was Hayden any good? Would I ask him? No, because he'd know I was spying on him. I refused to be that girl. Everybody needs an outlet and that was his prerogative just as long as it didn't affect me.

What was affecting me was my unofficial tour guide. I found myself wishing Lilly was there with me instead of having to pal around with someone who called herself Lorel Kanyun. I doubt Lilly had heard of SoWest because she would have worked her way into its sanctions long ago. It is super restrictive and invitation-only to join. Evidently Jerzy's invitation was lost in the mail. I thought, *Wait until Lilly catches wind of this.* Surely she'd say he turned them down. Our friendship kept me puzzled.

"What are you two whispering about over here?"

Hayden had either won or lost. By his demeanor, I couldn't tell, but I knew he was ready to leave.

"Oh, nothing…" I looked at Miss Kanyun and

winked.

At the elevator, I noticed a door a few feet away, leading to a small office.

"Since this is my first time here and all..." Taking hold of Hayden's hands, I took a few steps back gesturing for us to duck in there. "... I have to leave my mark, right?" I turned the knob behind my back.

"What do you have in mind?" Playing along, Hayden lightly ran his fingers over the front of my lace top, stroking my breasts and kissing my shoulders. Pressure from the cabinet behind me was uncomfortable, but didn't stop me. "You want to get caught, don't you?"

Hayden's kisses drove me wild. We were viscously engaged. I unzipped my skirt, letting it fall to my ankles. "Maybe..."

Honestly, I didn't think anyone had seen us. That was until...

"Well, lookie here... You need a hand with that?"

Hayden pulled back from our kiss, turning towards our audience. He smirked, and then with his foot, slammed the door in Lorel's face.

It was the happiest ending, ever.

~

On the drive home, Hayden noticed I was quieter than usual. Compared to my excitement when we got to the club, I was almost mute.

"Did you enjoy yourself?" He stared straight ahead as he focused on the streets and rolled through all of the flashing lights Downtown. "Uh-oh - what happened?"

"Lorel Kanyun, that's what happened!" I laughed, "She talked my freaking ear off ... and just then... What was that about?" I laid my head back; tired and full of alcohol.

"Yeah, I can't figure out why Tate keeps her ass around." Hayden reached over and held my hand. "I'm sorry about that."

With all of the questions in my head about Lorel Kanyun, and why she was sure she could get away with propositioning us, and the money Hayden blew on his extracurricular activities, it was moments like that which made those irrelevant. Hayden knew how to put me at ease. I was sure there were things I didn't know about him and probably was better off not knowing. But like I said before, as long as they didn't affect us, it wasn't an issue.

"Actually, she's not *that* bad. I've met worse. Tonight was pretty interesting. I'm glad we can get out and have a good time." I wanted to ask him about the money he lost, but didn't.

That kind of passive acceptance established the tone in our relationship.

When you're married to someone like Hayden, you're willing to do whatever it takes to keep him satisfied. In Hollywood, if a wife is not willing to play the role of his lover *and* his girlfriend, somebody else will.

I still believe that.

~

I woke up early Sunday morning, when I heard Sylvie in the hallway. Hayden was still asleep. Just before I opened the bedroom doors, I noticed the bathroom light on and went to turn it off. On top of one of the vanities was a hundred thousand dollars. In stacks, just the way I saw it at the club.

"I thought he lost."

When I asked about it at breakfast, Hayden told me, "My father taught me how to play poker when I was ten. It's fun!"

It's fun? He said that like he had won marbles. "You want me to deposit it?"

"Into the bank? Come on, Alex." He laughed, as if it was a foreign suggestion, and continued eating. "Okay, I tell you what... do what you want with it."

I mentioned the cash to Sylvie and she said, "Oh, he always wins, dear. He wins and just throws it in his closet. "He needs to respect money because it doesn't always last."

The kind of money Hayden had made me uneasy in the beginning. We signed some necessary documents when we were married and that was before I found out his Net Worth was seventy- five million dollars. That was a lot to take in, because I knew that people would assume I married him for his money.

Still, I took the hundred thousand and put it in the floor safe in *my own* closet.

I may have been passive, but I wasn't a fool.

Keeping up with the Joneses

*O*ver the next couple of years, Hayden and I were virtually inseparable. My own career had become nonexistent, though I convinced myself that I'd *chosen* to take a break to set up house. You know how that goes.

I completely catered to Hayden; making sure his life remained in order. This included running his errands, which sometimes meant driving him to movie sets in the early morning hours. The kind of things an assistant might normally do.

Keeping things *in order* included self-maintenance. I couldn't be caught dead being less than Hayden's smoking hot wife that the press loved. The pressure was heavy and I hated it. Especially after a photo was released, saying that I looked pregnant. My bi-weekly appointments at the Thibiant spa in Beverly Hills were staked out by paparazzi. They thought they saw a bump. *I was bloated, morons.* Still, because of that, I amped up my workouts with Jennar my crazy, militant fitness coach, and would go jogging in revealing, midriff-baring getups just so they would see my flat stomach. I had become a self-conscious and insecure mess. Trying to please the public by being the Jones they'd want to keep up with. I even began to resent Hayden because he'd brought this crazy life on me.

Then, just when I was feeling like an exiled house wife, Hayden would come up with the most amazing ideas. Like the one time just before awards season; he encouraged Lilly and me to take off and enjoy a week of spa luxuriousness – in Switzerland.

"Why don't you go on a trip with your girl, Lilly? I know you miss spending time together."

"Are you sure? I mean, you have so much coming up." I honestly felt guilty for *wanting* to get away for a while. There was part of the life I had before him that I longed for. He could sense it, so he gave it to me now and then.

"It's fine, baby." I loved when he called me baby because his voice was so sincere and I felt like the center of his entire world. "Besides, if you're not happy, how can I focus on any of this? You come first."

So off I went, to Geneva.

When Hayden wanted to keep me happy, he took care of my friends too. "If it pleases my wife, that's all that matters." That's what he always said.

Lilly didn't trust him. I could tell, but she played along for my sake and always showed Hayden a measure of respect.

She would eventually confess to me *why* she disliked him.

90077 - Feels like Heaven

*T*here was nothing about Hayden that was truly humble. The whole world loved him. He was one of the golden boys of Hollywood. Matt Damon has Hayden to thank for that kick-butt trilogy. Hayden turned it down to play a paraplegic educator who triumphantly took his fight for civil rights all the way to the Supreme Court. The role landed him an Academy Award nomination. Hayden spent an entire month living in the home of the real life man that the story was based on. I wish I had known Hayden back then. He told me that experience changed his life and made him feel good about himself and his career.

To say Hayden wasn't humble doesn't mean he wasn't appreciative and didn't have a heart. It's just the level of celebrity he reached, sometimes over shadows the person you are within. You start to believe your own hype, and you expect to be treated a certain way - by everyone. You *can* be too hot to be humble. Sometimes humility is simply not allowed.

That said, Hayden decided we needed to get "a better house". What that meant was to trade up to a more suitable home, so we could prepare for the family he wanted. That was just fine with me. Kimridge didn't fit us anymore. It had been Hayden's bachelor pad. We were now building a life together, so he gave me carte blanche on finding the house of my dreams. I secured a real estate agent and the hunt was on. I sought out the most posh and exclusive areas on the West side.

It turned out to be a thorn in my side; the pressure. You would have thought I'd be more excited about it all. Of course Lilly was eager to help me. She showed me the lay of the land, or as she put it, "The best that Hayden Jones' money can buy." After a month of parading in and out of mediocre celebrity enclaves, I found a house in Bel Air. Not a pretentious mausoleum, but a house I envisioned us growing into. When I brought him back to the eleven thousand square foot Mediterranean styled estate on the secluded and hedge-lined St. Pierre Road, we agreed it was home. Where our children would be born, love would reign and we would truly be a family.

It was just in time too, because right after moving in I found out I was two months pregnant. Finally, I would give my husband a baby. Of course, I was overjoyed about becoming a mother, but Hayden was over the moon. So much so that he announced it to the world during a late night talk show the next week. I wasn't happy at all about that because I wanted to wait until the first trimester had passed. Not to mention that neither of our parents knew.

Once again – pivotal moments in our lives, announced through the media.

Baby Watch

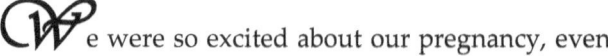e were so excited about our pregnancy, even though it was a surprise. Hayden, especially. He went along for most of my doctor appointments, regardless of the frenzy caused. He was on top of the world and wanted everyone to know. After months of persuasion, my parents finally agreed to get a house in the LA area. Like most, my father was so proud that he wouldn't let us buy the house, so I told him I *leased* their three bedroom house in Calabasas, until they figured out what they wanted to do. I got an earful when Paul Diamond found out I really had bought the house for him and Mom. But basically, I told my dad to get over it, because I needed them close by.

With my excitement, came the worry of difficulty carrying the baby or childbirth complications. It all terrified me because I'd been reading pregnancy books and had read so many stories on the internet.

By the third trimester, the paparazzi followed me wherever I went; and if it looked like I was shopping for baby clothes - forget it. Window shopping had become impossible. An amateur photo of me at the spa for my prenatal massage therapy ended up online. Paparazzi always seemed to show up at Babies "R" Us, right on time. Baby watch had spun out of control.

An afternoon, just three weeks before my due date, turned into gridlock on Robertson Avenue, during one of my shopping adventures. I recruited my occasional companion, Jeremy, who I met through Lilly. He's what they refer to as a lady sitter. It became too risky to travel out alone. We hung out shopping, lunching, whatever I usually did, including my spa days. Jeremy looked after me, in ways neither Hayden nor Sylvie had time to. He was great and took no mess from anyone. Not even Hayden, when it came to making sure I remained stress-free. Thank God for Jeremy because it had become impossible for me to show up anywhere without being hounded.

You'd assume wrong if you thought you could push Jeremy around. Metallic Chucks or not, he had balls and would put you in check. Robertson Avenue was packed with paparazzi that afternoon.

"You guys, get back – please! Hey you… get away from that door, or I swear!" Jeremy wrapped his arms around my shoulders and led me to the car parked just outside of the shop.

The shouts were relentless. "Is it a boy or girl, Alexia? … Baby names, yet? Come on - tell us!"

It was hard for me to understand why the press was

so hungry for this baby to arrive. There were early tabloid photos of my bump, and then full belly shots of me in a bikini, sunning by the pool. Paparazzi had to have climbed trees along the perimeter to get those. Baby gifts had been sent to the house by editors of magazines, hoping to schmooze their way into an exclusive after the baby was born. It all boiled down to money. Like there was a bounty on my baby's head.

When Hayden and I found out I was having a boy, we didn't feel obligated to name him after our fathers, or even ourselves. His name remained a secret. Our mothers were kept in the dark, for fear they would slip and tell a friend or family member who would leak it to the press for money. Very little was sacred, even amongst family.

~

"You feel it, that time?"

"I did... does it hurt?"

"No..." I giggled at Hayden's innocent sense of what goes on in a woman's body when she's carrying a baby. "...it almost feels like...tumbling butterflies, if that makes sense."

He laid his hands against my stomach fascinated by the baby's movement.

"Wow... that feels a little strange."

"Imagine how I feel, knowing a little boy is doing

back flips inside of me."

"What are we going to do when it's time?"

"Something tells me, when he's ready to make his debut, our instincts will kick in. I just wish he was ready now."

We shared a laugh, but Hayden was so worried about the kind of father he would be. He felt he needed to be perfect. I knew I wouldn't be the perfect mother. All we could do was vow to love our son and keep him safe and happy.

That was an easy promise to keep.

The promises Hayden and I made to each other... was an entirely different story.

Brooklyn

2am, Wednesday, August 11th

Week 37

"*H*ayden!" Alex cried out to her sleeping husband.

"What? Alexia, what is it?"

"My water just broke. It's no joke, seriously."

Hayden jumped out of bed and rushed over to Alex's side as she sat up, leaning against the headboard, trying to remain as calm as possible. That's when he noticed that her water had broken, all over the bed.

"Okay, so let me um… shit!" He grabbed the phone and called Sylvie's room. "Sylvie, it's time. Yes!"

"I couldn't sleep, so I walked down to the nursery and when I got back in bed, the baby kicked. And…." Alex glared at Hayden wondering why he was just standing there, and then saw Sylvie come into the room.

"Alexia, I'm about to call your parents. Can I get you anything, dear?"

"No, no….just my parents, Mareena and um… Lilly." Turning to Hayden and waving a hand she instructed, "Your mom has to get here, today." Alex's face grimaced from the slight pain. "Sylvie, can you go to my coat closet and get my Burberry trench, please? The long, tan one with the buttons...and also my shoes... Just pick a pair of Tory Burch's or Tod's - it doesn't matter. I can't go to the hospital in just a nightgown."

With his hands at his waist, watching Alex freak out, Hayden suggested, "Why don't you change if it's bothering you that bad."

Alex barked back, "What'd you think I was going to do?" Her contractions were approaching full speed ahead.

Sylvie chuckled at the comical pair. "I called Cedars-Sinai already and will call everyone else in a few. Also, I will bring your bag to the hospital. You two go...now, Hayden!"

Hayden snapped out of a daze. "Right! Baby, I've got you..."

After helping Alex change, Hayden got her to the elevator down the hall. Once they got to the garage, and into the Mercedes, it all hit Alex, and she started crying. "Hayden, our baby's coming."

"I know, babe." He kissed her face as she laid her head against the rest. "I love you so much ... you're doing great."

Hayden helped Alex settled into the back seat, where

she'd be out of sight. He raised the garage and backed out, dialing Kaz's number.

"Hello Hayden, what's going on?"

"Hey Kaz, it's early, I know, but the baby is coming."

"Oh my god. Now?"

Hayden laughed, "Yes, now! We're on our way to Cedars."

"Okay, so, what do you need? I'm getting dressed."

"Just uh, come down to the hospital. Alex will want you there and you can help make sure this stays quiet…for now, at least."

"I'm on it! Just find an Emergency nurse. Though, they'll probably find you first. You'll be taken straight to Delivery. Don't worry about the car. Leave it at Emergency and I'll move it. See you in a few!"

"Well, damn…" Hayden was shocked at Kaz's knowledge of the protocol.

"Hayden, I mapped this out months ago. Alex…can you hear me?"

"Yes …hi, Kaz…"

"We're getting ready to have a baby, girlfriend!"

Alex managed a soft giggle. "Thanks. Love you!"

Once at the gates, Hayden surveyed the scene before pulling onto the street. St. Pierre Road was quiet with not a car in sight. Relief swept over him, because the last thing he wanted was paparazzi tailing them to the hospital.

A grin crept to his face. In just a little while, his son would be born.

~

"Where is she?" Gabby rushed into the private delivery room, with tears in her eyes. "Oh, my girl." She leaned over her daughter, kissing her forehead.

Alex, was relieved that her parents had gotten there. "Hi, Mom…Daddy."

Paul was full of as much emotion as his wife. "My baby is having a baby. I never thought I'd see it."

Hayden hugged the Diamonds. "They said her contractions are only ninety seconds apart now. He's coming."

Just then, a nurse with a crisp British accent, walked in. "How are we doing here?"

"I will be better when this is over."

"Dr. Forrester will be in shortly, Mrs. Jones." Checking her blood pressure, the nurse assured Alex, "You're almost there, love." She turned to Alex's parents. "Good morning, you're Mom and Dad?"

"Yes." They answered in unison.

"It's a pleasure to meet you both. One of the attendants will show you to her maternity suite. You'll find it very comfortable as you wait."

"Oh! Mom, my friend Lilly should be here soon... and my assistant, Jeremy."

"Okay, we'll keep an eye out for them. Hayden...your mother called me and she's almost here."

"Thank you. See you in a bit."

Finally it was just Hayden and Alex, waiting to meet their son.

Alex had explained to her parents earlier that week that she just wanted Hayden in the delivery room when the baby was born. It's something she wanted to share only with her husband. Hayden told her she would regret it later, not having her mother in the room.

"I want his first moments to be with us. When we tell him about this later, he needs to know how much we wanted and loved him… from the beginning."

Dr. Forrester arrived. "Good morning, Mr. and Mrs. Jones." I think this little one is ready to meet his mom and dad."

"Feels like he wants to, right now…" Alex clinched the side of her bed, at the strong contractions. She refused the epidural.

The nurse and technicians were setting up. It was time.

"Okay, Alexia… I'll talk you through it all. You'll be just fine." Looking up at Hayden, the doctor could see he was just as nervous as Alex. "Keep her relaxed and focused, Hayden. Just like during your Lamaze, only this is the real thing."

The pains were elevating and Alex longed for the signal to push.

"Alright, I'm so ready!"

~

Brooklyn Xander Jones made his debut at 4:05am. His outcry echoed throughout the room. As Dr. Forrester pulled the baby out, Alex's lips tightened, fighting the burning pain. Even so, when she saw his head, she reached out wanting to touch her son, then instinctively grasped under his shoulders and pulled him the rest of the way out. Alex took hold of him, laying him to her chest. The nurse didn't cut the umbilical until a few minutes later.

Her voice barely above a whisper, she spoke to him, through tears. "Hi...hi, baby, I'm Mommy. I love you so much." She looked up at Hayden. "Here's Daddy..."

Hayden leaned close, with tears in his eyes, rubbing the baby's thick, slimy hair. "He is so beautiful." He couldn't believe life had turned out like this. That he had a family of his own. Kissing Alex's head, Hayden felt something in his heart that he'd never experienced. "I love you, Alexia."

"I love you, too."

Everything was finally perfect.

Baby Makes Three

*H*ayden became a new man when Brooklyn was born. He was now a father, and had never been prouder. It was heartwarming watching him melt in the presence of our son. We would parade around town as a family, at the beach or my favorite place, Beverly Gardens. Hayden even pushed the stroller to give me a rest, he said. He wanted the world to see him in Daddy mode.

When Hayden filmed locally, he would sometimes ask me to bring Brooklyn to the set. I loved when he included us in his work life. Sitting with the production team with headphones on, watching him become this other person, was so surreal. Unfortunately, those visits were always cut short, because Brooklyn would point and scream, "Daddy!" a little too much. It didn't matter if I had every toy known to man with me, Brooklyn wanted to talk to his daddy and he would cry when I tried to distract him. As cute as everyone found him... those little outbursts were very disruptive, and we'd end up hanging out in Hayden's trailer, which now had a play area just for Brooklyn.

We spent so much time together the first year of Brooklyn's life. Whenever Hayden was scheduled for production meetings or press events out of town, he brought the baby and me with him. The media turned up in droves during the New York press junket. When he did Good Morning America the hosts even invited me to, "come on out with the baby". To their surprise, I refused. Brooklyn's first year was fully documented as it was. It was too much. Hayden and I were enjoying parenthood and wanted to protect our boy, and be with him every minute that we could.

Mentally and physically exhausted, I wasn't always in the mood for anything extra and Hayden was busy developing a television series. Because of that, our sex life was hit and miss. Never had we gone more than a week without making love. Sylvie would urge us to go out for alone time saying, "I've taken care of a baby or two, you know?" I was confident that Brooklyn was fine with Sylvie. Still, it was hard for me to go out without him.

If I could bottle that time, I would have, because after that first year … things began to change.

Hayden: Faithful to the end?

$\mathcal{T}$he hikers at Fryman Canyon played nonchalant because in Hollywood you come across celebrities at every turn. But, Little Miss Screech didn't get the memo.

"Oh my god, Hayden Jones!" The young woman bounced in her sneakers with glee.

Hayden and his trainer Jake were in the midst of an uphill climb when they were intercepted by the bubbly jogger.

"Miss please, he can't..."

"I just wanna say hi." She ignored Jake. "I'm a big fan and... well, I can't believe you run up here."

Hayden, breathing deeply, put his hands at his hips, leveling his breathing. "It's okay, how are you?"

"I'm fine. Can I get a picture?" Not even big, bulky Jake's cock-eyed scowl could intimidate the girl. She rolled her eyes at him.

"Of course." Hayden waved the girl over and she huddled into his chest, sweaty tee and all, holding her cell phone up for the shot.

"Thank you!" She pressed her lips together, flipping her bottled blonde ponytail to the side. "Um, can I have a hug?"

Jake looked on, anticipating Hayden's next move.

Hayden grinned at her, as Screech's inflated breast seemed to point right at him. "Nah you don't want that, I'm all sweaty." He brushed her arm. "Enjoy the rest of your hike."

Miss Screech stood as dumbfounded as Jake. Well aware of Hayden's infamous playboy reputation, she was hopeful that he would choose her.

"Man, I remember a time when that chick would have been thrown in the back of your Range Rover and in and out of bed all in a two hour span."

Blotting his face with a towel, Hayden thought about that. "I would have back then. Come on, I don't have time for this, man."

"Wait, wait...hold up!" Jake in all of his sleaze, trotted catching up to Hayden.

Planting his foot on a big rock, Hayden glared at Jake. "What?"

"No, it's just...well damn; you're really faithful to the end, and all that?"

Flicking his sweat drenched towel in Jake's face, Hayden was over the conversation. "Well, if you had my wife, you wouldn't throw it all away to bone some random groupie!"

"Maybe, but still, I don't know how you do it." Jake dared to continue. "If all this free trim was throwing themselves at me, I'd be in divorce court tomorrow."

"Not if you love her. I'm not screwing my life up, brotha'." Hayden nodded as Jake's eyes followed after Miss Screech. "And, who the hell told you that girl down there would be free? Trust me man, none of these women come free."

In his mind, that meant not even his precious Alexia. He knew that if he was caught screwing around, it would end up costing him a lot more than a few tabloid headlines.

The pedestal

*G*rowing up in Barstow, I swore that I would never let a man treat me like a mindless robot. As if I'm not a partner, but just someone he's taking care of. The way my aunt Genevieve did. She married a businessman in Miami who pampered and put her on a pedestal, but she was always walking on eggshells for fear she'd disappoint him. They raised their two kids, and when they got into high school Aunt Genevieve went back to work as a pharmacy technician, part time. Mr. Business decided he needed her home after all, and walked into the job one day and demanded she quit. I was disgusted by it. Sure, what woman wants to *have to* work? But, it should be her right to. At least, bring it up for discussion and let me have input on what's best for our family.

Alas, there I was now, perched up on Hayden's pedestal. When we met, I was a thriving makeup artist and I loved my career. Just as major opportunities fell into my lap, I met and fell in love with a man who cherished me. I have no regrets about that. We were happy.

When Brooklyn was around two and demanded

more from me, something changed in Hayden. Not only did he desire the perfect family, but more so, it was up to me to remain his ideal wife and lover. In his eyes I should have been able to take care of Brooklyn and be at his beck and call the way I was in the beginning. It wasn't enough that Sylvie was there, and my mother was close by to take care of Brooklyn when we needed help.

"Alex, Brookie is growing so fast, and needs to get used to being looked after by other people. That's what these women do, and it'll give you a little break, right?" Hayden wouldn't let up. "You're his mother and will always call the shots, I promise. I just really need you to be available, especially now."

So – we brought on a nanny.

I have to admit, a couple of weeks in, Regina became a godsend. She was a maternal woman in her fifties and had worked with the likes of Madonna. Her reputation was impeccable and Brooklyn liked her. So, I knew he was in capable hands. Still, when he cried in the night, I was the one who got up... and I made sure that I was the first face Brooklyn saw in the morning. Super Nanny or not, I wouldn't give that power to anyone.

Having Regina on board freed up some time for me to revisit my own interests as well. A dream of mine was to start my own cosmetics line, focusing on eye shadows, liners and lashes. Mink lashes, like the kind Lilly wears, only faux mink. I wouldn't be able to stomach the real thing. It would take a lot of research and planning, but I held that vision in front of me.

I quietly talked to women in our circle that had successfully developed cosmetics lines, compiled ideas, and gained more motivation. I visited labs, met with chemists and manufacturers to learn the business. Fashion icon, Kimora, whom I had kept in touch with since my days of working Fashion Week, told me to make sure I was ready for such an undertaking, because I would only be received as seriously as I approached the process. I didn't want some fly-by-night line that came about only because I had the money to buy my way in; and then disappeared. This was a way to create something, on my own, born from what I loved.

Privately playing around with ideas, I got with a formulator who created two lipsticks for me, which I named Lexi Red and Lexi Nude. I was bursting to move forward the more I received compliments on the lip colors. Yet – I wasn't quite ready to start.

Brooklyn needed my full attention and quite frankly, so did Hayden. I don't know who required more. During that time, I became insanely insecure and that caused me to want to fix things. I wanted to spice up my life again, for myself and for my husband.

It was time to bring "Alex" back.

Hollywood approval

"*C*an you bring me some tea? No, change that...

water with lemon. Well, bring both... and, a long straw!"

I drove the medical assistant crazy. I was staying in one of our guestrooms, and was in so much pain that my neck was starting to throb because I held it stiff; afraid I'd trigger pain, or dislodge the drains. On top of pain, I was coming down with a cold and was scared to sneeze, which sent me over the flipping edge.

Day Two of recovery after getting breast implants.

I couldn't move because to reach for anything felt like pins were being poked into my chest. My breasts were wrapped so tightly that I was alert to every breath; every inhale or exhale. At the same time, the bandages eased the pain a little. I ate hardly anything, thinking that would reduce having to go to the bathroom.

Why did I subject myself to that? What brings a girl to the point of thinking that bigger tits will make her husband stay home?

My paranoia was rising to a ridiculous level; like I had never felt before. I heard and read all of the stories about my marriage in the tabloids and was subject to women looking at me with pity in their eyes, which made me wonder. It was an easy progression for that wonder to turn into belief.

One afternoon just before Memorial Day, Lilly and I were in Agent Provocateur on Rodeo Drive. The sales girl was being stupidly unprofessional. She seemed to be sizing us up as we browsed the delicate lace and silk garments. I ended up buying thousands of dollars worth of bras that I would rarely wear. I still had a bad habit of going braless; especially in my favorite cocktail dresses.

To my surprise, the girl had recognized me. While ringing up the sale, she confessed.

"Mrs. Jones, your husband is going to love these items, I'm sure." She paused recognizing that she was being too forward. "I'm sorry. I'm a Hayden Jones fan and he always exudes such good taste. I hope you don't mind my saying so."

Everyone seemed to know what my husband enjoyed, except me.

"Of course not." Actually, I couldn't have felt more uncomfortable.

Lilly jumped to my rescue. "Yeah, uh, thank you. What's your name, hon?" She leaned in to pretend to read the young woman's name plate. "You're pretty attentive and we so appreciate it." Her sarcastic tone was direct. Lilly didn't believe in over stepping boundaries. She was a hustler at heart and she knew this girl was being bitchy and nosey.

I saw something in this girl's expression that said, 'Poor girl, he's cheating on you and I hope your new bounty will help spice it up at home; to keep him there.' At least that's the sympathy note I read in her eyes. Actual or imagined.

She smiled, "I can have these delivered if you're continuing your shopping."

"Would you? That would be great." Lilly gave her a strong squint.

I was miserable and wanted to get out of there in a hurry.

What a damn fool I was. The writing was on the wall that Hayden was having sex with someone else. A woman knows.

My self esteem was sinking. *Maybe if I refresh things a little...* So I decided it was time to spruce up by calling on Doc 90210. Hayden encouraged it by saying, "You're beautiful just the way you are. That's why I love you." Then he added, "... but, it might be nice to have something extra to snuggle against at night." He thought he was being funny.

Inside, I wished he would have argued against it. Let me off the hook, but he didn't. Hayden gave me the green light, so under the knife, I went.

After recovery, I stopped hiding from the public. The press loved my new look, and so did I. Photos of me in cute sundresses playing with Brooklyn in the park, or out shopping, appeared in all of the gossip blogs and magazines. My clothes fit better and even my confidence was up. As for Hayden – I really can't say that he cared one way or the other. It seemed the more attention I got, the more resentful he became.

I was about to see that no matter what I did to keep myself in topnotch form, it wasn't worth my while, as far as Hayden was concerned.

The stage was set for me to be publicly humiliated.

Illusion by the shore

*T*here's a thick film smeared across Hollywood that makes the smog seem like cotton candy. The deception, immorality, the cons and thugs disguising themselves as film producers, agents and so-called friends; all the shady characters, including some of your favorite actors and actresses. You can't really trust anyone. At least you had better not be stupid enough to try. It's like Sodom and Gomorrah - on steroids.

I realized that I could no longer trust Hayden a hundred percent.

The beginning of my wakeup call came knocking one January Sunday morning. It was just after the Holidays and I thought we were in a calm, spiritually centered place in our lives. Brooklyn was almost four and he ran down the hall from his room, and opened our door announcing, "I'm coming in Mommy and Daddy!" Hayden told him he'd better start knocking so he wouldn't interrupt the wrestling games Mommy and Daddy play sometimes. This particular morning, Brooklyn came in and jumped on the foot of the bed. Then he lay down and went back to sleep.

I bounced my leg against the bed to wake him.

"Brookie, why are you down there, honey… you feel okay? Come on, you can sleep next to me." I sat up and pulled him up to the head of the bed, tucking him in, and feeling his forehead to check just in case he was coming down with something.

"I'm not sick." He looked up with squinty eyes. "Mommy, who's the man downstairs? I heard him, but Miss Sylvie told me to be quiet."

Man downstairs?

"What are you talking about?" Turning the light on above the bed, I saw the time was just after eight o'clock. "Hayden, who's here this early?"

Lying on his back and scrolling through messages on his phone, Hayden's demeanor told me he wasn't surprised. "Yeah, it's fine. Rusty sent him here to help me with something. It's okay, baby." Hayden got out of bed and disappeared to his bathroom. Five minutes later, he came out fully dressed and walked out of the room. "I'll be back. Love you, guys!"

Brooklyn and I must have been asleep for a couple of more hours when Hayden showed up like nothing odd had happened.

"Let's go to brunch." Hayden softly rubbed his fingers under my chin, being extra attentive, which made me suspicious. Still, I loved it. "Get Brooklyn ready and we'll go to The Ivy in Santa Monica. He loves it out there."

That was all fine and well, but where had he been and why was some strange guy at my house for my son to hear, before we even woke up?

The entire drive to Santa Monica, I pretended nothing weird had just went down at the house that morning. I barely noticed the two paparazzi across from The Ivy when we arrived. They had become a part of the landscape by that time.

Looking around the room, I didn't recognize anyone, which was nice because I could avoid any awkward chatter.

"You can order whatever you want, Brookie."

Brooklyn asked me to let him order his own food from now on. He was growing up so fast, and wanted to be like his dad. He picked up the menu like a little man, about to make a big decision.

"I want... two pancakes and the fruit on the side, with syrup ... the fresh kind."

Giggling, I assured him, "Honey, it's all fresh here."

The server was quick to respond. "Oh, I know what he means. I'll take care of it."

"My wife will have the Santa Barbara omelets. That okay for you, Alex?"

"My favorite..." I glanced up at Hayden hiding

behind those damn Tom Ford sunglasses, pretending no one would recognize him.

"And, I'll be having…"

"Banana French toast with strawberries?" The blushing waitress lost her professionalism. "I remember."

Hayden looked over his glasses and winked. "Right…"

Always one to special request off-menu, the servers never complained about it.

Rolling my eyes, I jumped in. "Let's have mimosas, as well."

Hayden didn't look up from the menu, "Of course."

Our server tried to play cool about the fact that she was witnessing a tense interaction between one of Hollywood's most watched couples. She flipped those menus around like a deck of cards, until I looked up and dismissed her. "Okay, we're good here."

Finally taking the sunglasses off, Hayden rubbed his fingers across my hand. "This is nice, I'm glad we came. It's been a long time since we've been out here."

Even though I had no real idea what was going on in his head, I saw him making an effort. Just the three of us, enjoying Sunday brunch the way we used to. For a moment, I was grateful to the illusion.

Hayden slid his hand away from mine. "So what do you guys want to do today?"

I smiled and turned to Brooklyn, "I don't know. What do you think, Brookie?"

"Can we go to the beach? I want to swim in the water."

Always willing to save the day for his son, Hayden jumped in, leaning towards Brooklyn. "You know what? We'll get a hotel right on the beach after we leave here." He looked over at me, grinning.

"That's a great idea!" I took out my phone and looked up the Ritz-Carlton. "A suite facing the ocean… but, Brooklyn, it's too cool out to swim." Brooklyn's faced dropped. "But, maybe…our suite will have a Jacuzzi, huh?"

"Yeah, cool!"

We spent two days on the beach in the Ritz-Carlton Suite. The same suite Hayden and I shared our first days as husband and wife.

Those uninterrupted days were the greatest high ever. Underneath, I knew something was broken, but it did not matter. Our family was together and Brooklyn was happy. Nothing else was important.

The illusion was the perfect escape.

Hayden, so, who was that strange guy?

Montecito, the week before

"*As always, it's good to uh, see you again.*"

Hayden was finished with his guest and tried to be nice about getting her out of his suite.

"*Right, playtime is over. I understand.*" *The fake accent rolled off her tongue and Hayden was aggravated with each syllable.*

The frustrated glance at his Rolex should have been the woman's cue to leave.

"*Good. My family is on their way and I'm meeting them, so if you don't mind...*" *Gesturing towards the bathroom, Hayden dismissed her and turned his back to the woman and started to doze off.*

"*Of course... and as always, thank you - and Alexia for that matter - for your generosity.*"

That was all it took. Hayden's eyes opened, as he whipped the covers back and sat up in the bed. "Don't ever say my wife's name. Now, get the hell out of here!"

"*I'm sorry. You don't have to be ill about it.*" *She snatched* her red laced *La Perla* robe off the bed and tip-toed towards the bath. "Hayden, you're going to look up one day and all of this will crumble right before your eyes..." She smirked and laughed as if she was in charge. "... then, what?"

Stressfully rubbing his face with both hands, Hayden was pissed. "Let me tell you something. If you think you just threatened me - you have me confused with those dumbasses you're used to dealing with!" Lying back on the bed, he dialed Alex. "Baby, how close are you to Santa Barbara? Good, I miss you. See you soon."

Rolling her eyes, the woman left in a hurry. She had her money, so didn't give one damn if the wife and son were coming to join Daddy.

As soon as he hung up with Alex, Hayden called his manager.

"Hey, Rust.... Yeah, you have to do something for me. Get rid of this girl. She's playing games, threatening to get to Alexia." Staring into the phone while Rusty convinced him it would be fine; Hayden got madder by the second. "I don't care if you have to send this bitch to Alaska, she needs to understand that Hayden Jones is not that sucker!"

At around seven Sunday morning, Rusty called his own private detective to pay a visit to the young woman Hayden had so carelessly paraded around Santa Barbara. He lacked the decency to keep her hidden; to protect his family.

Hayden might have slipped under the radar had he not taken her to an inn just one mile away from Sea Meadow, the gated Montecito community where he and Alex had purchased a seaside cottage just months before. Curiosity seekers and paparazzi alike, found out about the Joneses being the latest celebrity residents. It was a place their family could retreat to and relax, away from the bowels of Hollywood. And now, Hayden had gotten sloppy.

He screwed up and he knew it, so it was now cleanup time. That's where the private detective came in.

On that early Sunday morning when he showed up at the Bel Air house, he and Hayden paid a visit to the woman at her ritzy West Hollywood condo. After heavy convincing, she decided to move back to New York City; to be closer to Montreal, or so she told her friends. She was now a couple hundred thousand richer, so she kissed Hollywood goodbye. The woman also knew that if she didn't follow through and leave town, that Hayden's detective friend might do a lot more than bang on her door with an eviction notice.

Just like that, Hayden's mess was cleaned up.

Sleepwalking out of control

*T*he downslide of my marriage caught me off guard. I swore to myself that I would always keep one eye open and never let a man get the best of me; especially not Hayden. Wrapped up in my posh Hollywood lifestyle, I had everything a woman desired, at my disposal. But, I was a sleepwalker. Oblivious to what was really happening around me.

It became my own lazy fault.

Hayden was having at least one affair. I could smell it all over him. He had long started taking me for granted because he knew I wasn't going anywhere. In his mind, the birth of our son had secured that. "Your life is perfect" is what he would always tell me when I complained, or asked him about some rumor. I heard that so often from him that I pretended to believe it.

That's when the meltdown started. Deliberately doing anything that would bring negative attention to my life. Somebody needed to see what we *really* were.

I started going out alone, partying with strangers in nightclubs, was drinking more and allowing the paparazzi to follow me; even beckoning them to. Giving them all of the condemning photos they needed. I wouldn't go out until late at night, and because I knew Sylvie would make sure the house was locked down, I felt like I was still being a responsible mother.

One night after I put Brooklyn to bed, I went to a private party in Malibu. Lilly offered to pick me up but, I insisted on driving myself. I needed to clear my head and she would ask too many questions along the way. So, I met her at The Colony.

Everything got completely out of control.

The next thing I knew, I woke up in Lilly's guestroom. My clothes were strewn over a chair; apparently after she put me to bed to sleep it off.

It was getting bad.

"Whose house was it? I saw Vin Diesel there, didn't you?"

"He wasn't at the party, Alex."

"Well, some fake wannabe was there!" My head spinning, I sat back down onto the bed. "Lilly, sometimes I wish I hadn't come to Los Angeles."

"Alex, are you alright? Let me get you some coffee."

Glancing at the clock on the night table, I panicked. "Why did you bring me here? Hayden's going to go crazy!"

"You were drunk and lost control, that's why!" She

shouted back with that judgmental look all over her face. "What are you doing, Alex?"

"Nothing, but I have to go!"

I got dressed in a hurry, and ran out of that house as quick as possible only to realize when I reached the driveway that my car wasn't there.

Lilly drove me back to Malibu where my car was in the circular drive of the party house, untouched with no evidence of what happened - I thought. That's when I noticed the rose bushes I had plowed down. Apparently, I rolled back into the flower bed with my car, trying to drive myself home. Lilly took my keys and left the car there.

It was around eight in the morning. My phone was dead and I could only imagine that Hayden was furious and would want to throw me out. It was fine for him to stay away all night, but if his perfect Alexia did it and word got out, well…that just wouldn't work.

When I got home, Hayden wasn't there. I found Sylvie coming down the kitchen steps in a robe with coffee in her hand. Without a word, she fixed a cup for me too. Sylvie just watched me with those suspecting eyes. She asked no questions, but something in what wasn't spoken, told me she already had the answers.

Messy Montecito

If you're going to cheat on someone, at least extend them the courtesy of not getting caught with your pants down. Also, not taking another woman to what used to be "our slice of Heaven" would be smart as well. Montecito was *our* place and Hayden loved it so much that he risked sharing it with at least one of his hoes. Not whore - hoe.

The most degrading moment of my life came when a photo of Hayden, hanging out at a hotel in Montecito, was splashed across Kipp Dash's gossip blog.

I wouldn't have expected the media to care about his family, but I thought Hayden would care more about Brooklyn and me. He had lost all respect.

In the middle of a nap one afternoon, I got a call from my mother. It was right before dinner. Hayden and Brooklyn were outside, in the pool. When I answered, Mom's voice nearly knocked me out of bed.

"What is going on over there, girl?"

"Mom, what are you talking about?" *She's finally lost her damn mind.* "Where's Dad?"

"Never mind Dad. Where's your husband and why

aren't you taking care of that household? Keep your family out of the news!"

"Don't say that to me! I have no idea what you're talking about, but..." Suddenly a text came through. It was Lilly. "Just a second." Lilly's text read *Sweetie, are you okay? Is Hayden there? Call me now!!* "I have to go. Bye, Mom!"

Whatever was going down was now scaring me. It was no coincidence that my mother and Lilly were frantically reaching me at the same time. Sitting in the middle of my bed, I called Lilly.

"Honey, are you okay? Where is he?" Lilly made no sense.

"I should be asking what's wrong with you and my mother."

"You seriously don't know..." I heard her mumble *Oh my god...* under her breath.

"Look, I'll call you right back, okay?" I rushed her off. "Right back." I didn't want to hear it from Lilly, but I knew my worst fear was about to be confirmed.

I ran down the hall into the office and did an online search of Hayden's name. Hearing Brooklyn's laughter over the balcony, I dreaded what I'd find. I could feel the thread of my life unraveling and if it was broadcasted anywhere, I'd find it on Kipp Dash's site. I had to find out before Hayden did. The wife is always the last to know.

The story showed a close up of Hayden's face, and then another of him standing on a terrace facing the so-called mystery woman who was donning a halter top, with her back to the camera. She was no mystery to me. That trashy bitch. The caption read: *Hayden, that's NOT Alexia!*

It was sickening, and mostly because I knew exactly what had happened.

By that time, the paparazzi had grown on me. Probably because my old photographer buddy (you remember the one from my exit at The Ritz-Carlton, when I was a happy newlywed) was at the helm of the public interest in me. I was certain I'd need him on my side one day and sure enough, though I wished that day hadn't arrived - it did.

We were about to spend a week in Montecito since it was the Holidays and Hayden had a two week break from filming his television series. I loved when we went away because it was the one place Hayden was relaxed and not so pressured, having to brush Brooklyn and me off because of meetings or an early call to the set.

"I'm going up early to spend some time with my mother. It's been a while since we've had our time. You know how she gets."

At that time, Hayden and Mareena were having a tough relationship. I wanted him to bond with his mother. So, he left for Santa Barbara and Brooklyn and I were going to meet him at our cottage in a couple of days.

Playing that week's scenario in my mind, my body went numb and my heart froze. I refused to give Hayden the satisfaction of me making a big scene and a fool of myself.

I wasn't surprised by any of it. It was the confirmation that hurt so bad.

Crying, I called Lilly back. "Lilly!"

"Oh my god, Alex, I'm sorry, honey!" She heard the beeping in my car as I got in. "Where are you?"

I tossed my handbag on the passenger floor. "I'm leaving the house, right now." I kept Lilly on the phone, and kept bawling. "He's such a bastard and he doesn't even care!" I saw the paparazzi when I drove out of the garage. "Oh my god, they're all over the street!" Paparazzi were waiting at my gates. I opened them and sped through. Not giving damn if those gates stayed open or not. "This is so screwed up!"

"Tell me where you're going, Alex!"

"I need to think, but I don't know where to go." That's when I remembered the one person who would hear me. The irony. "I'll call you later." I wiped the tears away.

My car sped towards Mulholland Drive. I needed to hide from the press and from Hayden.

"Hello, Geoffrey? It's Alex. I'm nearby and was hoping I could stop." I couldn't hide the fact that I was crying.

When I got to Dr. Geoffrey's he was waiting for me in the driveway. Opening my car door he didn't ask any questions. Just knelt down and held my hand while I sobbed against the steering wheel.

"My life is a mess. I don't know who to trust."

"Of course you do. That's why you came here."

The Good Doctor

$\mathcal{A}$ good cry and cup of herbal tea later, Dr. Geoffrey was everything I needed. It had been years since the Venus shaving experience and honestly, I missed his straight forwardness.

Geoffrey was always someone I could turn to, throw my issues on, or not. Sometimes I just needed to hide.

Regardless of the circumstance, to run off to another man's house was irresponsible. I do know that. But, I didn't have many girlfriends to turn to, outside of Lilly, and even with her it was risky. Lilly based her core decisions on what people owed her. No one owed me anything. I just deserved to have some peace in my life now and then.

"Just hear me out, Alexia." Geoffrey sat next to me on the sofa, taking the cup out of my hands, and held them. "You have to go back."

"How can I?"

"He's been calling your phone. Obviously Hayden knows the shit has hit the fan."

"That's the only reason he's calling."

"Forget about Hayden. You go home, because your son doesn't need to be punished. At least go home and be with *him*. Think about your situation."

"So, you're saying that I can't stay here."

He chuckled. "True, because I don't need some crazy movie star kicking my door in." Geoffrey was able to bring a smile to my face. The good doctor kept it very real. "You have to go back home Alexia... tonight."

"Why should I? If anything, I'm relieving his burden. If he loved me he wouldn't have slept with that skanky piece of trash!"

Looking at me like the naïve creature I was, Geoffrey grinned and shook his head. Nothing was funny and I felt like even he wasn't taking me seriously. My head was spinning like a twister.

"You don't believe that." He sipped his tea and broke it down to me. "Listen, I don't know your husband, apart from the guy in the movies, but he's a man. We don't screw around because we fall out of love." He leaned in to deliver the dirty truth. "He did it because he could."

"What?" That made no damn sense. "I'd rather he fell out of love with me!" I fanned Geoffrey off and snatched up my purse. "I know you're trying to make me feel better." My heart was literally aching. "You're right. I need to see Brooklyn. That sweet little boy got dealt a bad hand in the parent category."

"He's why you have to stay with Hayden, for now."

He kissed me on the forehead. "You'll work this out, Alexia."

Any normal woman would have wanted Dr. Geoffrey to make love to her and sex her woes away. I know he wouldn't have pushed me away either, but I needed someone like him to remain in my corner for the right reasons. If I had tricked out like that, any respect and sympathy for me would have gone out the window.

Back to Bel Air, it was. *Hear his side and make sense of all of this. Make this work, Alex* is what I told myself.

Just to show you

It was week two of working things out. Who were we fooling?

I poured myself a glass of wine. "Want some, babe?" It would have felt so good to dash it all in his face.

"Alex, what are you up to? And, don't play with me or I swear…" that nervous vein throbbed in Hayden's neck.

I cut my eyes in his direction. "You swear what? You have some nerve." Continuing sipping, I laughed off his arrogance. It's like he still saw me as that blushing, blinded-by-love fool that he'd married. Hayden grabbed my arm, clutching me with his might, causing my Tiffany bracelet to dig into my wrist. "Get your frickin' hand off of me, Hayden! Are you crazy?" I snatched away, slamming the glass on the counter.

Realizing what he was doing, Hayden held his hands up. "Sorry… my fault! I can't even talk to my wife anymore without all of this dramatic bullshit. You better let this go, Alex. Your life is perfect, but it could get a lot worse - trust me!"

I was tired of faking and pretending that we could go

back to being the apple of each other's eye.

"Dramatic? Please – you didn't have the decency not to take her to Montecito. That's our place... and don't you dare threaten me!" I felt every ounce of blood flowing through my body, angry at the nerve of him trying to scare me straight. "I have been with more than my share big egos and huge wallets. So don't get it confused, you're not the first!"

He glared at me like I was dirt. "I'm sure I'm not. But, you just remember...whatever you're *assuming* had better stay in that pretty little head of yours."

"Assuming? That's funny, because you KNOW I know exactly what happened. Now it's all over the blogs, baby!" Seeing the look on his face when I said that felt great. "So screw you - I don't care! You got caught for the whole world to see. And, just to show you how much I don't care – I'm leaving your ass!"

Swiping my hand across the island, I slammed the glass to the floor and it shattered into pieces. Stepping over it, my focus was getting out of that house and away from Hayden. He was driving me crazy and the only chance I had to hold on to some sanity was to leave.

I cherished the fact that I held onto my Rossmore apartment. It was my sanctuary, my haven away from the Hollywood garbage that I had become used to; even felt comfortable in. I had to force myself to grab onto the reality I knew still existed somewhere. Now and then I would drive to Hancock Park and remember what it was like before my life became so complicated. Hayden felt as if he owned me and that was killing me. I swore I'd never let that happen; let a man have that kind of control over me. So, I packed a few bags and left - without so much of a word to Brooklyn. Our world had fallen apart and at that moment, I wouldn't do either of us any good. I couldn't think straight so I walked out.

~

A week had passed.

"Alexia, come home baby, because this has gone on for too long. You made your point." Hayden's voice spoke out of my cell phone. "Call me and let me know when we can expect you. I have a meeting tomorrow and Brooklyn needs you here."

No remorse. He wasn't sorry, but needed me to come back home and mend the broken fences.

I just couldn't go back. Not then.

Hollywood 101:
Being the wife he needs

$\mathcal{W}$hat drove me insane about my marriage were

the games. I left Bel Air that night in a devastating rush. As for Hayden… he didn't even call me at all for a week.

When I called to speak to Brooklyn, I was told he was not available. But, I know Sylvie was behind Brooklyn calling me the second night I was gone, asking why I was not there with him. I just told him that Mommy needed to go away for a little while and promised that I'd be back. My heart hurt telling him that. There had to have been nothing but confusion running through his little head. Of course, I blamed myself for dividing my household. I consumed just about all of it.

After Hayden's message, I received a call from Sylvie.

"Alexia, will you be coming home? Brooklyn is asking for you. And, you have the Golden Globes coming up, you know. You two need to work this out, dear." Clearly, Hayden put her up to it, but still, sincerity rang out in Sylvie's voice. Was this woman as crazy as we obviously were, or was she truly trying to save us?

Though I dreaded seeing Hayden and listening to the lies, there was only one decision.

Hollywood girls don't cry

"*Y*ou promised me on our wedding night that you wouldn't do this to me!"

"I made a mistake, Alex. Come on, anybody can slip!"

Anybody…can…slip. Those words made me feel numb and worthless. Destroying our relationship was a slip up?

You know that moment when you start thinking back to when you met the love of your life, and all of the romantic times you shared, the magic you felt in their presence? All of that flowed through my mind as I watched Hayden standing in the mirror drying his sculpted body. When I returned, I tried to put the cheating behind us. But him suggesting that I was overreacting and even imaging half of it… that was unforgivable.

"It was no slip. The only regret for you is getting caught." My hands were trembling so much that I could barely buckle my stilettos. "It's fine. I don't want to talk about this anymore, because it's pointless."

Triumphantly throwing his hands in the air, "That's just what *I'm* saying, Alex."

Hayden closed the French doors to his closet, as if we were finally agreeing. Inside, I vowed to never let him forget what he's done to us.

I didn't know how I would make it through that evening.

It was the Golden Globes and the press and fans were waiting to see if I would be on Hayden's arm; supporting my darling husband. His television series, The Stunt Job, was nominated for a second year. As executive producer, it would be a huge honor for him if they won.

Ever the Hollywood girl, I put on my best face and sexiest dress, because I was still the wife of Hayden Jones, Hollywood Hero, and I had to dazzle his audience. In his world, that was part of my job. So I sucked it up, because Hollywood girls don't cry.

Hayden gave me a smug-ass pep talk on the red carpet. "Cheer up baby…every girl out there wishes she were in your shoes."

I wanted to grab E! News' microphone and announce to the world what a jackass my husband was.

The Stunt Job did win the Golden Globe. My role as the supportive wife was carried out.

The next week, I moved back to Rossmore and was there for four months. This go 'round, he didn't seem to care. Why? Because I was at the house every day, would cook dinner and sometimes stay overnight, as if everything was back to normal.

Our seventh anniversary was approaching and you guessed it; Hayden talked me into returning.

This time though, I warned him: "If we start down that road again, and I leave, that's it. I'm marching straight into the lawyer's office."

Hayden didn't take me seriously.

A Hollywood finale to end all others

Bel Air: Night of Hayden's and Alex's anniversary

$\mathcal{A}$lex had returned home just in time for their anniversary. Hayden called and begged her to come back and work things out. "We put too much into our relationship to throw it away, Alexia." As usual, he was convincing.

It was a disaster.

~

"I should have never married you, Hayden! You have completely ruined my life!"

"Then get OUT!" Hayden yelled at Alex, standing there in their bedroom doorway with his hands resting on the frame... eyes glaring at her. "Either be the wife that I need you to be, or just leave Alexia, and this time don't even try to come back."

Hayden had become so cruel.

At that moment it was a stretch for Alex to remember the way he had loved her. She stood there dumbfounded over his audacity of giving her an ultimatum. She had decided enough was enough.

"I swear, I hate you!"

Alex stormed off and ran into her dressing closet, grabbing clothes and stuffing what she needed into Louis Vuitton carryalls, with as much disorder as her life had become. She then went down the hall and started packing Brooklyn's things.

Hayden pushed the door open with so much might, that it smacked the wall; forcing a hole through it.

"Don't think for a second you're taking my son out of here! You should know better."

"Why are you doing this to me?" Hot tears streamed down Alex's face as she pleaded, "Hayden, please! I can't leave him again, but…"

"Then, you know what you have to do, don't you?" He calmly turned and walked away.

Clinching at her chest, Alex was drained of everything. "Oh my god, I can't live like this. I can't…" Breathing deeply and sobbing, her vision became hazy and nothing made sense, as Brooklyn's clothes fell from her limp hands.

Brooklyn appeared at the bedroom doorway. "Mommy, what's wrong? You're crying?" He was nervous because of the shouting.

Alex turned around, went and knelt down, rubbing his face, "It's okay, baby. I'm just tired." She lied. "Hey, your pool party is tomorrow. Make sure everything is set up the way you want it, okay?" She held a strong front for Brooklyn. "Go find Miss Sylvie. Go on, now. I love you!"

Every part of Alex's body trembled, causing her to stumble against the wall as she returned to her bedroom.

"I just need to get out of this house. Things will be better." She convinced herself, turning on the faucets to run a bath. She undressed as she approached her closet. Opening a drawer, she pulled out one of her lavish sleeping gowns. Alex loved silk; the way it felt against her skin. "If I can just get Hayden out of my head for minute..."

~

The taps at the door didn't penetrate Alex's attention at all. Then Brooklyn's pounding became more furious. "Mommy, are you still in here? I need to ask you something." Brooklyn turned the knob, entering his mother's bathroom.

Fear filled his little soul. "Mommy!"

He ran out of the room and down the long hallway. Tripping to the floor, Brooklyn got up and kept on until he found his father in the other master suite. "Daddy!"

"What is it Brookie?" Hayden saw terror all over his son's flushed, tear stained face. A look he had never seen. Kneeling down he asked, "What's wrong, Son?"

"Mommy's hurt." He desperately pulled at his father's arm. "Daddy!"

Hayden broke away from Brooklyn and ran down the long hallway, bracing himself. When he walked into her bath he found Alex slumped sideways in the tub, arm dangling over the ledge, dripping a puddle of blood. He looked at the marble ledge and noticed that somehow she'd jimmied the blades out of a shaver.

"Alex, oh God - no!" Kneeling beside her, Hayden took his cell from his pocket, frantically dialing 9-1-1. He saw her chest heaving up and down, but she was growing pale. He quickly grabbed a towel and wrapped her wrist. "What have you done to yourself?" Emergency answered. "Yes! Please, my wife - she needs help. She's… had an accident." He lied, knowing this was no accident.

Hayden gently pulled Alex from the tub and onto the floor, covering her with the silk gown that was draped across the chair; her head resting against his legs.

Alex came to. "Nooo…what are you doing?" Crying, she slurred, "You never loved me …" She could barely move, but tried to pull away, as Hayden held pressure to her wrist with towels. She passed out again.

Just then Sylvie appeared at the doorway. "Hayden? What in the world has happened to her?" The crimson smears stood out as soon as Sylvie peered into the bathroom. A housekeeper looked on behind her.

Hearing Sylvie's voice and knowing Brooklyn was on her heels, Hayden threw his hand up and instructed, "Sylvie, keep him out of here!" She turned and head Brooklyn off at the pass, taking him to his room.

Shortly after, the Los Angeles Fire Department paramedics came rushing through the bedroom doors. Hayden looked on from a corner of the room, but caught one of them watching him with a judgmental glare. Even in the midst of tragedy, Hayden was worried that people would wonder what could have driven his wife to this emotional collapse. Surely, they would blame him.

"Mr. Jones, is there anything else you can tell us about what happened here?"

Hayden just stared at Alex's limp body on the floor. "Um, no… only that my son found his mother with her wrist opened."

"Right. Well, she also took at least a few of these." The man held up a bottle of valium. "She's stable and we're taking her to UCLA."

A few minutes later, Hayden watched Alex being carried out. Panicking and not knowing what to do, he realized he couldn't just walk into an emergency room full of people and fill out paperwork after his wife had just attempted suicide. He dialed his assistant.

"Kaz, I need you to meet me at UCLA Medical's parking lot. Yes - right now! It's Alex." Hayden sighed. "She ... she really hurt herself this time."

"What'd you say to her? She would have never..." Kaz went silent. "Okay, I'm on my way!" He hung up.

Hayden stared at the floor, thinking that it sounded like Kaz was already blaming him.

Brooklyn would be traumatized for life. He had just witnessed the most horrific scene of his young life. Hayden knew enough about Alex that she hadn't intended for Brooklyn to find her like that, so he would do whatever it took to make sure she was okay, even if just for their son's sake. Hayden still loved Alex, but he wasn't sure if their relationship could ever recover.

His team of spin-doctors would have to work overtime to clean up this one.

In Hayden's selfish mind, Alex had gone too far.

ACT III

Becoming Ex-Mrs. Somebody

Too much

couldn't handle it.

I had just turned thirty. My life had become a spiraled mess and it was time to face it. *How did I end up here?* Questions flashed in front of me and I was afraid, ashamed and not sure if I could climb out the dark hole.

You know how you try to avoid looking at something that reminds you of the worst moment of your life? No, I'm not recalling how Hayden smashed my heart to pieces when he cheated on me.

Those bandages on my wrist were constant. What would have happened if Brooklyn hadn't come in? As much as I hate that he saw me like that, it was a miracle that he found me in time. Mommy's baths are never interrupted. It was a rule because that was my private escape. But that night, I was desperate to stop the pain. It had become too much to live with.

The only thing I remember was waking up in UCLA Medical and being told that I wouldn't be going home because I needed help. I had really made a mess of everything, I thought.

Being in a rehabilitation facility was torture.

Those three months were like being locked in a coffin. I felt like I was dying because there I was again - without my son. I could only imagine what he was being told, and there was nothing I could do about it.

Celebrity Wife survival

*H*ayden visited me only five times at Sanctuary Ranch; the spa-like rehabilitation facility in Sonoma Valley, where I was receiving extensive psychiatric therapy. His visits were like scolding sessions. Mind you, because he was within earshot of staff, my beloved movie star hubby would always throw in an 'I love you Alexia and I want you to get better - for Brooklyn and for us.' Reading between the lines I knew what Hayden was really saying was *Pull your yourself together so that we can work it out because if you tarnish my reputation anymore, you won't be seeing Brooklyn anytime soon.* In this town, Hayden had the power and I knew it, but I focused on getting back on my feet and not let him control the game anymore.

It would be a long road. I was trapped and had reached the breaking point.

Brooklyn was allowed to visit me just once when Hayden asked Sylvie to bring him. He knew that I was sick, but couldn't understand why Mommy couldn't get better at home, with him. How do you explain that to a five year old?

I held Brooklyn in my arms as we sat in a lounger on the patio of my suite. We were dressed similarly, with me in one of my many Juicy Couture track suits, and he in his school warm up suit. He was growing so fast and was becoming quite a little athlete. We talked about school, and that Hayden had been teaching him to play golf at home.

"I'm not that good, yet."

Combing my fingers through his mass of curls, I was so proud of him. "Well, that's alright. You'll be better than Daddy soon. You'll see."

"Yep."

I managed a smile, but there was an uncomfortable pause. For me, anyways.

"Brookie… here, turn around. I want to see you." He rotated around, sitting at the edge of the lounge chair, as I crossed my legs underneath me. "I really miss being at home with you. You know that, right?"

He nodded, looking down, fidgeting with his wristband. "When are you coming home?"

"Soon, baby." It was time for an attempt at apologizing for scaring him the way I did. We squeezed each other's hands and it was killing me inside. "I'm so sorry, Brooklyn…" He waited, with those big eyes staring up at me. "… and, I will never…ever, do anything to make you scared again, I promise."

"Okay." He squeezed my hands tighter.

I grabbed him in a hug. "I love you so much!"

"I love you too, Mommy. Oh yeah… I made something for you but, you can't know until you come home."

"Really? Not even a hint?"

"No, it's a surprise."

"Alright…"

Brooklyn would be fine.

A child psychologist regularly visited with Brooklyn at our house and according to Hayden, "Brooklyn is a strong kid and just needs you back home." Strong or not, he was only five and should have never witnessed his mother trying to die. Those scars will last forever. Hayden was always thinking of himself.

Luckily for me I became friendly with another famous spouse who I'll dub **Celebrity Wife.** She is married to one of the most successful television and movie producers in the business. **Celebrity Wife** opened up about the passive-aggressive relationship with her closeted husband. She gave me insight on what I was about to face and that I needed to get well, get out of there and back in Brooklyn's life, before Hayden poisoned his mind against me.

Celebrity Wife's suggestions weren't always tops, but she was right. I had to look out for myself. In Hollywood, sympathy for the wife of a star lasts only as long as their picture perfect persona as a couple. After that – she's on her own. It's sink or swim and I was not about to drown.

My life had turned into a nightmare, because I was gullible enough to believe that when I married Hayden, the scales would be balanced. Now, the public would assume I was bad for him. *Look what she's done to him. Why did he marry her in the first place?* Still, listening to **Celebrity Wife**, who in her own right was listed as one of that year's Fifty Most Beautiful People, talk about walking in and *almost* catching her husband in the act and continually being threatened by him with 'you didn't see anything…you'd better think again…' and him trying to convince her that she's insane when she knows what is happening around her, made me reevaluate the way I was dealing with my situation.

I didn't want to end up like **Celebrity Wife** who was clearly bearding a gay man who didn't love her. She just fit the part and he needed her for the time being. Now, there she was in her third stint in rehab because she drank, snorted and shot up her way down those red carpets. It was **Celebrity Wife's** way of surviving.

Her story was an eye opener and I knew I had to fight to get better to change my life; a life that would no longer mean being Hayden's robot. He had become toxic to my wellbeing and though I still loved him, I wanted out of that marriage as quickly as I could. It would take some time, though. I had no plan, no idea when or how I would manage it, but if I wanted to see light at the other end, I had to work on myself and get my strength back because it would be a hard fight.

~

My psychologist had some serious work to do if she wanted to help me. I was feeling hopeless. My self-worth had bottomed out.

"Alex, did you hear me?"

Dr. Val was more patient with me than I could ever be with myself. She sat legs crossed in her wrap dress, in a lawn chair across from mine and waited for a response.

Gazing out over the rolling green hills, I was in another world. Thinking about Brooklyn and what a mess I had made of our lives.

"Yes, of course, um…I just… I need to get back to my son. But, Hayden…"

"So? What about Hayden? You're Brooklyn's mother."

Dr. Val pulled her glasses off and placed them atop of her head, pushing her perfect bob behind her obviously pinned ears.

"It's not that easy." *Why doesn't she understand this?*

"Okay, so we're going to forget about your husband for a minute and focus on Alex. You're going to build yourself up. You ARE strong, even if you don't realize it."

"Strong? How is it strength, when I consumed all of the blame and felt dying was the only way to fix things?"

"How did this start, Alex?"

I turned attention back to Dr. Val. "What? How'd I let Hayden drive me crazy?"

"Alright, if you wish…"

"I gave it all up for him: my own dreams, who I am, my friends - all of it. I got lost because I became the Wife Of, just the way he wanted."

Dr. Val watched me talk, curled up in that chair, being Alex, the victim.

"So, now you know that. But Alex, you've been here these past few months putting in the work… for your son. This is no longer about Hayden. You're taking that power back."

Tears spilled from my eyes as I imagined Brooklyn's life going on without me. I didn't know if he still missed me or was getting used to Mommy not being at home. That's the part that worried me.

I came to an awakening that it wasn't possible to live peacefully in my current state. Hayden and I were no good together. When I left Sonoma Valley, I stayed at our house for a couple of weeks. If nothing else, it was a shield from the press. They couldn't get anywhere near me behind those gates, and I wasn't concerned with what people were saying on the outside. Miss Sylvie took care of me. It was almost like having a mother there. My own, even though she visited me, always had disappointment stamped across her face. Being back with Brooklyn built me up. He gave me the air I needed to build my strength. Still, I no longer wanted to be around Hayden, and I avoided him as much as possible.

One morning while Hayden was still away on location in the desert, I had movers take as many of my things out of the house as possible. I stored it at Rossmore until I could figure out what my next step was.

The only thing I knew for sure was I was finished with being someone's emotional punching bag. Sylvie and I sat down with Brooklyn and explained that she would take care of him for a little while, when I wasn't there. And, that I was trying to make it easier for all of us. He seemed to be okay when I told him, "Daddy and I can't live together right now." There was no doubt that Brooklyn would be okay.

I left hours before Hayden was to return.

As promised, that was the last time I moved out of the Bel Air house. If Hayden had been listening, what came next was no surprise.

Served

Paramax Studios Lot

"ayden Jones?"

Sitting in the director's chair, Hayden shot back, "Yeah, who is it?" Craning his neck around in frustration of being interrupted, he wondered what this person wanted.

The envelope nearly smacked his shoulder. "You've been served. Good day, Sir." The suited up young man half smirked and walked away triumphantly.

"This shit is not happening!" Looking around for his assistant, he excused himself from the set. "Kaz, get over here!"

~

After those soul searching sessions with Dr. Val, I built up the courage to divorce Hayden. There was about to be a mudslinging war, and I knew that. But I needed out, because if I stayed, I'd end up dead the next time.

I knew better than to snatch Brooklyn away when I left. I also knew that Hayden would be able to keep him safe, where I wasn't sure if I could at that point.

My attorney tried her best to talk me out of leaving my son, but there was no convincing. She couldn't understand why I left Brooklyn there, until I finally said, "If I had just taken Brooklyn from the house, Hayden's lawyers would make sure I never saw him again!" Hayden was powerful and his bulldogs would make me out to be this drug addicted head-case, and I'd lose Brooklyn for good.

True, I was the one who filed for divorce, but I counted on my attorney to fight the battle. I didn't have the strength. Brooklyn needed both of us, so I danced to Hayden's tune for a while, just to see Brooklyn and to eventually get everything I deserved.

In hindsight, I know it could have all blown up in my face. But, I was tired of walking on egg shells. It was a chance I had to take, to reclaim my life.

Hayden squared

*H*ayden showed up pounding the door of the apartment with so much anger in his voice. What he said was not just hurtful, but terrifying. I couldn't help but feel like I had made the wrong move.

Oh my god! "Hayden, what are you doing here? Get away from my door!"

He banged on it with a fist. "Alex!" Then he stopped. It was pin drop quiet and I stood there, afraid to breathe, for fear he might hear me. I couldn't tell if he was still there, but I was sure he was. Next came the shift. "Alexia... Alexia, why are you doing this? Because of that... whatever her name is?"

"Don't you try and play me. I'm not stupid!"

"I messed up. You know how much I love you, baby. You're my life. You and Brooklyn are all that matters. The rest of this shit means nothing."

There he had returned. Hayden Jones - the tender man that I fell in love with. Where'd that other person come from? It was like dual personalities. Not just one for his public and one for home, but like two completely different sides to Hayden - which only I got to experience. He was so tangled up, that he had lost all cool. And then, to lose control of his household – well, that was not allowed, so it pissed him off.

I didn't dare open the door. My neighbor across the landing greeted him. Hayden yelled at that poor man and ordered him to get lost. It was completely embarrassing. But, I thought *now they see*. Our dirty secrets were unfolding. Hayden was no one's hero that day.

"Hayden, you've got to leave me alone. I'm not coming back!"

"Fine - don't, then." I peeped through the hole and saw him straighten up, like he'd been leaning against the wall at my door. "You'll be begging me, I promise you!"

Just like that, he left.

What did he mean by that?

Speculating over what Hayden's next move was terrified me because I knew it would involve Brooklyn.

McQueen would not approve

*I*t was a scorching, sunny Friday afternoon, and Melrose Avenue was crawling with locals and the usual tourists taking pictures while hoping to run into someone famous. Hidden behind sunglasses, there was no chance of anyone recognizing me as Hayden's wife. I was tired of the sympathetic expressions I got at the spa or the local coffee shop. I seriously considered doing all of my shopping in The Valley. No one bothers you there, unless you're a Jackson.

There was time to kill before meeting up with Stacee, so I tried engaging in some retail therapy at Alexander McQueen. I got a text from Stacee letting me know that she was parking nearby. I changed my mind about the items I held in my hand, and decided to just head over to Taste restaurant. The sales associate's attitude sucked anyway, so it gave me an out, and I didn't feel bad about it.

I looked at her with a scowl. "McQueen would not approve of your lazy ass!" I tossed the scarves back towards the shelf and walked out. May he rest in peace.

"So Stacee, we haven't talked in ages." I pushed my fork around the plate, shoveling the cobb salad I wasn't eating. "What's going on, girl? Tell me all about Paris."

Stacee had been out of the country for over a year.

"London."

Glancing up, I found Stacee looking at me like she was wondering why I was being evasive about what was happening with my marriage. "Paris...London...that's what I meant!"

Stacee frowned at me.

Throwing my hand up to my face, I started crying uncontrollably. "I'm sorry. It's gotten so bad and I don't know what to do."

Stacee grabbed my other hand. "Sweetie, just... try to relax. I can't believe this is going down like this. You guys were so happy."

"I know, but that's just it... I don't know if he was really happy or I just fell into the timing for his plan of Perfect Wife, Perfect Life."

"Nooooo.... Hayden loves you. I was there from the beginning and saw how he beamed when he married you."

"Then what happened? Because it wasn't a buildup. He's not the same person. It was like... suddenly he became *this* guy."

"I don't know, but Alex, I care about both of you... and it breaks my heart knowing what you've been going through."

Stacee was in Europe when my meltdown or suicidal crisis as the tabloids so entertainingly described it, occurred. She missed all of the messiness.

"I'm not trying to make you choose sides, it's just… I have no one I talk to who cares anymore."

"What about Lilly?"

"I know, but Lilly can't stand Hayden. She never liked him and can't be balanced at all when I ask her for advice. Now that she and Jerzy have broken up, she's turned into someone I don't want to be around. Lilly told me, 'I knew Hayden would do this to you. He was too much like Jerzy; calling the shots.' That hurt me so bad. Plus, she's going back to Vegas anyways, so…"

"Wow…" Stacee waved the server over, "Oh, do you mind, Alex, I need a glass of wine, right now. - You?"

"No, I'm good!"

I nursed my cranberry juice, while wishing I could have a drink, but I vowed not to. It scared me to even think of having a glass of wine. The flashbacks, one in particular, of me and alcohol were horrid.

Hayden had gone to bed especially early on this week night because he had a five o'clock call on set. He didn't need me tossing and turning next to him, nor would he have noticed I wasn't there, or so I thought. I went to Brooklyn's room, and told him one of my favorite stories until he fell asleep. It was something I did all the time. He loved my stories. The ones my mother told me when I was a child. Once he was asleep, I tiptoed out of the room, and pulled the door up. Brooklyn was three years old at the time.

Sitting in the hot tub and enjoying a smooth Pinot, my boredom turned into madness.

I changed into one of my least mommy-like dresses and by eleven, when everyone was good and settled for the night, I took off in the Porsche that Hayden had been zooming around town in. My car wasn't wicked enough for what I had in mind. I felt alone when Hayden was working nose to the grindstone, because he shut me out, saying he couldn't get emotional and that it would throw the character off. That mostly left me out. So I took off, headed towards West Hollywood.

I pulled up at Hyde and the line was deep, so I definitely had an audience. Why not put on a show? The guys moved the cones and let me park the Porsche up front. The doorman opened the door and reached for my hand ushering me inside, where security marched me to a roped off table next to the DJ's booth. I wasn't a fool and knew that I needed to be guarded even if I was rebelling against my husband.

The music was pulsing and I stood up dancing and flirting with the crowd, as if no one would know who I was.

Some random party girl shouted up at me, "Alexia! Is

Hayden coming?" I ignored her.

"Hey, Alexia, girl!" Some very pretty boys were yelling my name from the dance floor. We synchronized our dances to the thump of The Pussycat Dolls.

I had grown used to people recognizing me, but knew they were really just hoping to schmooze with my movie star husband. I usually got away with murder if he wasn't there. No one cared what I was doing. After all of those years, I was naïve enough to believe that. I asked my server to go get the boys, so that I had people to hang out with. She returned and while I ordered bottles of champagne, up popped Monet Caprice's rent-a-ass, of all people.

"Alexia, how are you, honey?" She craned her head around, "Wait a minute, Hayden let you out of the house, alone?"

"He doesn't LET me do anything, Monet. But I'm fine, how are you?"

"Oh, God…" We exchanged fake kisses. "I'm fab. Working my fingers to the bone." She shrugged and smiled, holding a champagne flute to her glossy lips.

Raising my brows, I knew what that meant. "I bet!"

"Girl, it's been so long, hasn't it?"

"Since when… since you've seen me?"

"Well, yes. What else could I mean?"

"I guess." Gesturing towards my new friends, "We were about to have a drink, to celebrate, sooo…" One of the boys caught on to my wanting to get rid of Monet.

"Girls night out! WhooWhoo!"

I winked at him. "Right! – Good seeing you Monet, take care!"

She gazed at the guy, and rolled her eyes, as she walked away.

"We saved you, girl!"

"Yes you did. Thank you."

We partied for an hour or so and then I left them to the table full of high priced spirits and champagne. Staggering in my McQueen stilettos, I made my way down the long hallway to the front door.

The doorman approached me and whispered, "Are you okay? I can call a car for you."

"Noooo… I'm fine. I just live fifteen minutes away."

Thinking I was doing well, as I drove up Sunset Boulevard, the lines became blurred.

I remember waking up in Cedars-Sinai with Sylvie standing over the bed in the observation room in Emergency.

"Sylvie, what's going on?" I grabbed her arm in panic. "What happened?"

"You were in a car wreck, dear. That pretty little car… not so much, now."

"What?" I felt fine. How was that possible? The first thing I thought of was Hayden being furious. Why couldn't I *have gotten back home without this shit happening? A police officer was standing just beyond my door and turned back, looking at us. "Does Hayden know?"*

"He sent me here. Alexia, you were drinking far too much tonight. You bumped your head against the window, and the front of the car is smashed up. That car swerved and slammed into a fire hydrant on Sunset Boulevard, in Beverly Hills. You could have been killed!"

Sylvie sat there and scolded me like a child.

It felt like a bad dream or a joke to teach me a lesson. It wasn't – because a couple of hours later I was at the Beverly Hills police department- processed for a DUI. I called my attorney and was allowed to go home.

In all of his haughty disappointment, Hayden didn't speak to me for two days.

There were huge fines and hours of classes. Then the worst being the court assigned community service: janitorial work in the women's division at the Twin Towers Correctional facility downtown. After being called 'prissy-ass-bitch' and every other vile name in the book, by inmates and guards alike, I would have rather been locked up. After four months, my driver's license was reinstated.

And for the record - No matter what the tabloids said, I did not purposely slam into that hydrant.

"Well, all I can say is… just make sure you keep yourself together. Don't give anyone reason to make you look like a bad mother, because Brooklyn needs you. Even you said he wants to live with you now." Sipping her merlot, Stacee mumbled, "This is beyond messed up..."

"Yes it is - you have no idea!" I tried to liven up, but my life was so real that it killed any glimmer of a smile.

Hayden and I needed to figure this out. I wasn't about to let Brooklyn suffer because of our mistakes.

Ice Storm in Century City

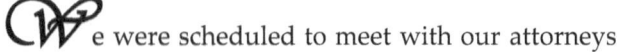e were scheduled to meet with our attorneys and the social worker. I hadn't heard from Hayden since he almost kicked my door down. But, I wasn't scared anymore. That fear had evolved into determination. Hayden was using Brooklyn as a pawn and it was hurting me, so I had to make my voice heard, even if it failed.

Hayden walked into the room and right past me without so much of a word that afternoon in Century City. He was punishing me. That boardroom felt like a freezer. We had become as strangers. No matter, I wasn't letting him treat me like dirt anymore. The mediator gave me a chance to speak first. Hayden refused to even look at me, but he heard every word.

"I had so much love for you. I was willing to do *anything* you wanted. Anything you required of me. I forgot who I was; the girl you fell in love with had long vanished. I became weak and needy and insecure. I guess that's what you wanted, I don't know... What I do know, is I won't *give* my son to you! You can take everything from me, all of the bullshit stuff. You just cannot tell me I can't be with my son. You tried your best to make him hate me and I think he may have for a while. But, now…now he sees. He sees, and he wants to be with me and you can't keep us apart!" I started to cry and my attorney handed me a box of tissue and I pushed it across the table. "I don't need that! Hayden, I never make you out to be the bad guy in his eyes, no matter what you've done to me, but you're not going to shut me out. Not anymore."

"Are you done?"

All I could think was *the audacity!* To treat me like disposable garbage. I got up, walked out and let the attorneys hash it out. Whatever was meant to be would be. As risky as that was, I couldn't take it anymore.

Later, my attorney came to my house with the parenting agreement that was proposed. Hayden's side didn't contest *any* of the terms. We were both shocked that he had signed it.

The agreement was to joint legal custody. That's what I wanted the entire time. I didn't want Brooklyn to not be with his father. But, I wasn't going to let Hayden walk over me.

As for the property and money - that's what I hired Gillian Alfonse for. The silver haired, infamous family law attorney, who was nicknamed "The Black Widow" by the media, would not let Hayden stiff me on what I had earned with my blood and tears.

Hayden ain't right

*H*ow in God's name could I have made the right decision to divorce Hayden, when it included not seeing Brooklyn every day? I had convinced myself that it was best and that I was being responsible. Even though we all knew that Hayden was a whip-cracking sonofabitch.   Still, I had to show him that I could stand on my own again, and not head back down that dark path of self-destruction. He was losing his power over me.

Part of that recovery was finding a place to live that was a hundred percent fresh. I let go of my Rossmore apartment. The memories were too strong and the energy was suffocating. Kaz, our mutual ally, found me a three bedroom hillside house to lease in Benedict Canyon, where I stayed until the divorce was final. He went out on a limb, but Kaz insisted on helping me, and felt bad about how everything went down. No one knew Hayden's ways better than Kaz. I assured him there were no regrets over him introducing us that night, because I now had a beautiful son from it all.

Oddly enough, my husband never cut me off

financially. I'm sure he thought I'd wise up and run back to him because he was the gravy train. There was close to a half a million dollars in my personal accounts when I filed for divorce. *Plan for the just in case, because things happen* was my thinking. So, I socked some away, so to speak. I had signed a post-nuptial agreement and it never crossed my mind to argue against signing it. It was unavoidable and Hayden would have been a fool had he not presented it.

What I had on my side was the baby. I'm smart enough to know that Hayden probably would have left long before I did, had it not been for Brooklyn. That's how his mind worked. He started joking that I was the girl who stole him from the others. Who says something like that to his wife? I remembered when I was the girl he fell in love with and needed.

As the years went by, I believed Hayden stilled loved me, but was no longer interested in being a husband and staying true to what that meant.

~

His mother called me the night of my storming out of the meeting with our attorneys. When her number came up, I braced myself for another smack in the face. First from Hayden, and now his mother was chiming in.

"I know you probably don't want to talk to anybody, especially not me, but...

"Mareena, I can't do this. Please…"

The last person I wanted to fight with was Hayden's mother. I was sick of being blamed, threatened and yelled at.

"Alexia, please just listen to me. Two minutes – that's all."

I sighed. "Okay, fine."

"I'm not taking sides. I do love my son, but I love you like a daughter. Now – that said, he…" Mareena paused and I could almost hear her words being lined up. "Hayden ain't right. I know it!"

"Why are you saying this, Mareena?" As usual, I was so confused by her words.

Mareena was sobbing. Either from her afternoon mixed drinks or she was hurting over the whole divorce situation. It was hard to tell with her. "Because there's so much that you don't know about him. He shuts everybody out. But believe me, this is killing him. I'm his mother and I can't reach him when he's like this. Still, I know that he loves you. Just be a little patient with him, and try to understand."

"Understand? What are you talking about? I almost died dealing with him, Mareena! Do you understand *that*?"

"Sweetie, yes, I do … Oh dammit, this is coming out

all wrong." The sound of ice clicking was prominent.

"Don't try to explain anything for him. I love you for it, but…" The conversation was upsetting and pointless. "It was wrong from the start. We were a mistake!"

"No you weren't. My grandson is no mistake!"

"I hear everything you're trying to say and I appreciate it. But … I really have to go."

"Alright…" Mareena's voice was hollow. "You're going to always be my daughter-in-law, you hear me? No matter how this turns out."

"Okay, Mareena. I'll talk to you soon."

As I hung up, sadness swept over me when I realized that I received more sympathy from Hayden's mother than my own. My father on the other hand, wouldn't even mention Hayden's name in our conventions, he was so upset. Daddy blamed himself for approving of someone who would go on to cause me harm.

Not my mother. To this day, it's my fault that I *allowed* my marriage fall apart.

We still have a long way to go.

Hayden: Make it right

When I met Alexia I hadn't counted on falling in love with her. I admit, that when I saw her standing in my living room all alone, studying that painting, I had decided she would be with me. Something about her was different from any woman I had been involved with. Of course she knew who I was, otherwise she wouldn't have been there, I'm sure of it. But, she was real… and a little afraid to let me get too close. I also knew she'd set me straight if I tried anything. That piqued my interest. I had to find out what she really was about.

Being with Alexia was the first relationship where I could try and be myself. The jury is still out on whether she deserved to know the real me. I didn't even want to.

My life is full of nothing but opportunists. Even the people who claim to have my back are in it for something. Their loyalty is based on my longevity as the prize horse, the breadwinner and the one who keeps them relevant. Everyone except for Kaz, maybe. He made it clear from the beginning that he was not a fan, thought I was cocky and a bit of an asshole…but I could see in that kid that he was smart as a whip and extremely organized. He was the person I needed because my life was chaos. I went through assistants, sometimes two at a time, like shoes. They couldn't handle the job. The status drew them in, but not the responsibility. Kaz has been here for years and is literally my right arm.

Alexia was the missing link in my personal life. She *gave* me a life - and of course, when I felt what happiness was about with someone I truly loved... I screwed it up. I'm starting to think my mother was right about all of this. She asked how the meetings were going, and then she let me have it.

"How could you do this to her, Hayden? That girl gave you everything! Alexia gave up her career and dedicated her soul to you. You've got to stop this pattern because you're doing this on purpose." I turned away but she grabbed my face with her hands. *"You need to figure this out, Son."*

"Figure what out, Mom? That I'm so destructive that I can't allow myself to have someone like her?"

"It's like you sabotage every slice of goodness that comes into your life. You work yourself to death, make all of this money, and don't trust anyone to stay when they get to know the real Hayden Jones — so you destroy it before they do."

Listening to my mother roll off my idiosyncrasies, I thought, I should be paying her instead of my over-priced shrink. I had no choice but to accept what my mother said because she hit it dead on.

"*She's never going to come back to me. But still … I owe Alexia. This almost killed her.*"

With tears in her eyes, my mother begged me to make it right.

It was time for me to be the man that my father would want me to be.

I knew right then what I had to do.

Make those lessons work for you

Hayden called me on a Tuesday morning.

The finalizing of the divorce had dragged out for almost seven months. Before this, he had refused to meet with me privately and would barely utter a word when I would come to pick up Brooklyn or drop him off after our visits together.

Then, out of the blue Hayden called and asked if I wanted to pick up Brooklyn a couple of days early. He also said he wanted to talk to me, without our lawyers. Of course, I rushed right over.

When I got there, the housekeeper met me at the door and this time the greeting was more pleasant than usual. It felt like a trap.

"Mr. Hayden is on a conference call, but he wanted you to know he'll meet you in the kitchen. Feel free… whatever you like, Mrs. Alex."

Normally, this woman barely acknowledged me when I came for Brooklyn, and always stopped me at the entryway.

I paused, looking at her puzzled-like. Wondering what kind of sick set up was this. And, now the damn staff was in on it. "Okay, well…thank you."

"Of course." She walked off humming some song or another.

It felt good to be back in the house I'd helped decorate. Looking up that double staircase, I wondered if any changes had been made to our master suite; if Hayden had completely erased me from it. And, worse… whether someone had already taken my spot.

I shook those thoughts off, and went to the kitchen. The first thing I noticed was the amazing note on the chalkboard I put up for Brooklyn before I moved out. The message read *Don't forget. Mommy is coming today Daddy.* Evidently Hayden told him I was coming earlier than scheduled. He was still at school.

I fanned the tears out of my eyes when I heard Hayden's steps approaching the kitchen. Turning around, I didn't know what mood he'd be in. There was no telling.

"Alexia, how are you? " That's when I noticed his arms were a little more buff under the caps of his sleeves, but I digress.

"Fine Hayden, and you?"

"Not bad. Not bad at all. I'm sorry… I had to finish up that call. It's crunch time before production and I leave for Dubai in two weeks. You know how it gets."

We exchanged a friendly smile.

"Yeah, I know." I quickly went over to the Sub-Zero and poured myself some lemonade. "May I?"

"Alex come on, this is still your house." He pulled a stool out and sat, watching me.

"So, what's really going on, Hayden?"

"Alex, this is getting out of hand. It's time to stop it!"

"Stop it? What do you mean? You're the one who…"

"Woman, if you would listen." He cocked his head at me as if I was put in time out.

"Fine!" I gulped back the lemonade and discovered it was bland. I was willing to bet Brookie had made it. My healthy child hated putting sugar in anything. That's when I noticed Hayden sliding a black leather folio across the island. "What's that?"

"Just take it home, review it and let me know if you're agreeable and we can let these guys know we're done with all of this. Then maybe we can move forward with our lives. Brooklyn doesn't need this, Alex; us fighting back and forth. I think you'll find it fair. As your girl Lilly would say, you've earned it all."

Damn right - and fair? I'll bet.

"Can I look at it now, if that's okay?" I flipped through the pages of the documents. Then came to a screeching halt when I saw the Settlement Agreement page and what Hayden was proposing. His attorney must have choked when he saw *Five Million Cash,*

Twenty-three thousand per month in spousal support, thirty-two thousand per month in child support and a new home of her choosing (within forty miles of Los Angeles County)
"Hayden, is this for real?"

He got up and poured himself a juice drink from the blender. "It's not a joke." He chuckled as he took a sip. "Alex you're Brooklyn's mother and I still love you. I just wish I could…"

"It's okay." I walked away from him, trying to catch my breath.

Hayden` followed me, catching my hand.

"Alexia, please… I'm trying to say I was wrong and I'm sorry. For everything."

Staring in his eyes I flashed back to our first meeting at Kimridge Road, to getting married in Hawaii and finding our dream home to my suicide attempt then to the present. How did we get to such a bad place?

Looking down at our hands, I noticed he was still wearing his wedding ring. Fighting against tears, I pulled my hand back.

"I appreciate that – so, what time is Brooklyn coming home?" Walking over to the breakfast table, I sat down. My emotions were all over the place. "Look – I'll review it with my attorney but, I'm pretty sure it's fine. Hayden, thank you."

"I mean, I'm not going out like some of these guys leaving the mother of their children high and dry so she has to end up selling her story."

"That's what this is about? You know I wouldn't do that to you. It's not my style!"

"No, no I didn't mean it like that. I just want you to be okay for the rest of your life."

There was a genuine remorse that I had never seen before. Something then told me that when Kaz helped me all those times, it was Hayden who put him up to it. When someone has emotional power over you and they know it, the savior complex kicks in to make them the hero. Talk about inner demons.

~

Hayden took a turn for the better after our divorce was final. It was like the noose was loosened and he returned to being the guy I first fell in love with. Hayden resented me towards the end of our marriage. Had he felt tied down? He rushed *me* to the altar, not the other way around. Placed me on this pedestal only to kick it down. But now – remorseful Hayden had appeared.

"We mutually decided that this was best for our son. He's a wonderful father, and I will always care for him." - End quote.

That has and will always be my favorite comment to

the press. The least I could do was defend him over our breakup; especially since it was me who laid out the bread crumbs for the blood hounds.

"That's right. We'll be at the Montecito house all week, but my husband will be there a couple of days ahead of me. Don't trap him, you hear me? – No, you heard me. I know how this works. All you do is wait...point...and click. – Right! Because if he sees you and throws something at your ass... Hey – that's your bad, my friend!" Okay and thank you for signing that little agreement. If this goes down the way I think it will, we don't know each other after this. Alright - goodbye."

My husband made me look like a fool. Every salesgirl from Beverly Hills to The Valley knew what was going on. I wasn't about to snoop around myself, because my heart would burst and I'd probably flip the hell out and end up kicking Hayden's ass in the streets. So I called on my paparazzo pal.

The sad thing was, I honestly didn't expect him to get much. But, when I saw the images of Hayden and Monet together on a hotel balcony, it almost killed me. Initially thinking I'd be relieved either way, it backfired on my heart. Though I pretended, there was no way in the world that I could stay with him.

That's why I filed for divorce.

Our marriage was over. We both had come to terms with that. Still, despite it all, Hayden and I became friends. We had never really had that while married. For the first time, I saw his vulnerability and even began to understand him better. It's very odd to say that, but it's true.

I'd had enough of living in the city, and found a beautiful four bedroom house in North Ranch Estates in Westlake Village. The property backs up to the golf course and Brooklyn loves being out here. He tells everyone, "We live in the country!" I suppose we do, compared to the hustle and bustle of Los Angeles. We have a pool and spa and our own putting green and we even take horse riding lessons. It's an oasis.

I have finally found the peace I longed for.

Now and then, Hayden spends time with us here in Westlake. It's a long drive from Bel Air, and when he brings Brooklyn for his weeks with me, what can I say? I don't always run him off. That crazy chemistry we had didn't completely die with the marriage.

I truly loved Hayden and I always will. The tragedy is that our passion played out too quickly and it was all downhill from there. But now, we have respect for each other from the heart and I will always have his back. People always ask why I don't hate him for what he did. Call me naïve if you want, but Hayden is Brooklyn's father and I see my son in his eyes. I could never hate that.

You never know what you're getting when you become involved with a celebrity, but overall…I still feel that Hayden and I were meant to be in each other's lives – in some form.

In Hollywoodland you had better not expect anything from anyone. Sometimes, life comes at you out of left field and you have to stand tall and take the blows. Then, make those lessons work for you. My old friend Erik was right about that.

All of those years, I was dying to make it to Hollywood, and then almost died getting out.

I've started over - taking care of myself for a change. Not being emotionally dependent on Hayden or anyone else. And, you know what? Alexia Diamond-Jones is not the same girl who got off the bus from Barstow almost ten years ago. I'm a lot wiser and am enjoying my own life and success.

You've heard of Diamond Eyes Cosmetics, right?

Being a Hollywood Ex is tragic only if you allow it to be.

As for me - I choose to be happy.

*

www.ingramcontent.com/pod-product-compliance
Lightning Source LLC
Chambersburg PA
CBHW032142190626
46814CB00005BA/1803